THE SCREEN **SAVERS**

You can find out more information about
The Screen Savers here:
www.bryanromaine.com

For additional fun, for various benefits, and to make me
look popular, follow me on my other social media sites
too – including these ones:
www.facebook.com/BryanRomaineAuthor
www.twitter.com/bryanromaine
www.youtube.com/bryanromaine
www.instagram.com/bryanjromaine

#TheScreenSavers

THE SCREEN SAVERS

BY BRYAN ROMAINE

This is a work of fiction. Any similarity between the characters
and situations within its pages and places or persons, living or
dead, is unintentional and co-incidental

A CIP catalogue record for this book is available
from the British Library

Book Cover Design by Mecob
Cover images © shutterstock.com

www.bryanromaine.com

Thanks to

Thanks to Martin Ouvry for his editorial input, to Mark Ecob for his book cover design, and to the following people for their many kindnesses in helping me put together this novel:

Justine Solomons, Stewart Trotter, Caroline Goldsmith, Kay, Jackie Shearer, Marc Blake, Antonio Rochira, John Rice, Nathan Veerasamy, Tim Dendy, Anji Clarke, Ric Beesley, Anita Shah, Nick Rippington, Ian Sutherland.

For Vic Beesley

1

Meeting: 2001

Adam likes spending the afternoon in the cinema, where he can be alone – think he's alone at least. He'll sit at the front watching *Bamboozled*, a Spike Lee film. Nobody goes to see his films, not around here, not in the day – it's like his own private cinema.

He asks for a cappuccino and is given white coffee. He does not cause a fuss. The cinema hasn't quite understood the whole speciality coffee revolution. It's got a machine with lots of sticky labels: 'cappuccino', 'latte', 'espresso', 'decaf'; but they all produce the same thing – white coffee. They do, though, have nutmeg, and chocolate, and are ahead of their time in many ways. They have other toppings, like hundreds-and-thousands, small chocolate Flakes (20 pence extra) and chocolate crunch (an all-sort mixture of chunky bits of chocolate that he suspects are 'pick and mix' crunched up: chocolate mutants past their sell-by). Once, he'd had the crunch and a crushed jelly baby floated to the surface – so the crunch is not all chocolate, or all crunchy. It shouldn't even be called topping, because it sinks: the bits are far too heavy, what with them only serving white coffee with no supportive foamy top. You're left with really sweet coffee and a sticky mess at the bottom of the cup which is impossible to get at. It can't be dug out – they don't provide spoons. No. If you actually want to eat the crunch, you have to take a mouthful of chocolate, add the coffee, and gargle.

Oh, there is a spoon. Adam uses it to dish out the crunch. But it is chained to the desk.

He takes his coffee and pays for it. He slips a Flake into his pocket without paying – call it compensation for the cappuccino fiasco – and enters the screening room. It's empty: what a relief.

He sits in row four. The bottom section: the flat bit at the front. He's never known anybody but him to sit in any of the front section of seven rows – well, almost nobody – not for a small film like this. Of course, yes, people sat there for blockbusters, after six o'clock and at weekends, when the seats in middle and back are, say, fifty percent full. Oh, and school holidays, how could he forget school holidays – some kids like to sit at the front and get neck-ache. This is a pain for him too. If they sit at the front so must he. And, yes, he too gets neck-ache. (There's a big difference in degrees of head–neck elevation between row one and row four, a surprising variation for, what, ten feet in seat-to-seat distance.)

He likes all styles of cinema – low-budget, art film, foreign and mainstream. He enjoys the less mainstream films for reasons which include the additional pleasure of an empty screening room. (In this cinema, off-peak, any-way.) Screen Seven. That's where they show that kind of material – anything non-mainstream. They show them in bouts of one to two weeks. Last week, a low-budget called

The Martins; today it's *Bamboozled.*

They dim the lights very slightly and the adverts begin – they vary the degree of darkness as the main feature gets closer, as if they're trying to add to the tension (or allow people to find their seats – that's another reason). For the adverts they dim, but you can still make out the pattern in the ceiling, quite a lot of light really; for the trailers it gets a lot darker, you can't see any pattern. And for the feature, you lose all perception of ceiling, as if it no longer existed. There's just blackness. Could be to infinity. Could be to ten feet above the screen, where it was before the adverts, when they play radio.

During the second advert, a woman walks past and sits in the first row. Right within his field of reality.

He checks – centre and back seats are empty. The cinema, apart from the woman, and him, is full of space.

There are five seats in row one. She sits in the second, one seat from the aisle.

He moves past her, and sits in seat four (he'll not sit at the end of a row, for reasons he keeps to himself).

This time it is she who looks around, and notices, too, that the cinema, apart from them, is still empty.

'I'm not a lunatic,' he announces with some confidence.

Pause.

'I know,' she replies with equal assurance.

Another pause. Advert number three finishes – there are usually four adverts for a film like this.

'I've seen you before,' she says.

An awkward pause.

'I'm not a lunatic either,' she continues.

Leaning across their dividing seat, she tells him she likes to sit at the back. That she comes to see films on her own. Thinks of it as being *her* cinema, this screen number seven, where they show the less mainstream films. Only he's always there, sitting at the front, and though she's accepted him being there she just wanted to see one film sitting at the front, with nobody else ahead.

They watch two adverts in silence. Two adverts during which he finds himself distracted, first by the pattern on the ceiling, which has now, given his new head elevation, become far more distractible, then by her coffee – which he imagines she'll slurp through the entire film, but is sipped quietly, with some grace, and is finished by the end of advert four.

She puts the cup down in the cup holder fixed to the seat next to him. An empty cup but for its mushy chocolate bottom.

'What did you have?' he asks.

'Latte.'

'And chocolate crunch?'

'Yes,' she replies, then quietly: 'but I didn't pay for it.'

He could see how you could get confused – the '20 pence extra' sign hangs over the Flakes, but you could easily presume it applied to all toppings. He doesn't mention it.

'Well, you haven't eaten it yet.'

'No,' she says. 'You got a spoon?'

'No,' he says.

They spend some time conversing about the coffee-making facilities and the benefits of various sitting locations within Screen Seven – a subject matter of which his knowledge is limited to the first few rows. While talking, the adverts finish and the trailers start.

'Why don't we both sit at the back? It's like sitting at the front but you feel you're in a bigger room,' she says.

'Yeah?' He takes a look at the back of the cinema. The

room is still empty. Really empty. Sometimes, when he went in and sat near the front, he pretended it was empty when he knew very well that a few people had come in after the trailers. He hadn't seen them but could hear their rustle and blocked it from his mind. Once, he had turned around to see four people in the middle seats; they too had stayed on until the end of the credits. There had been popcorn also, covering the gangway, crunching under foot as he left, evidence that there had been others who'd left before the credits had finished.

The chances of their being invaded now, though, are low: the film is about to begin; trailers have finished; opening credits are rolling.

They move towards the back, sitting next to each other with just the one seat in between, and watch the movie.

Halfway through the film, Adam would confess to be enjoying the proceedings. Sitting in the middle towards the back is proving to be an exhilarating experience and he is able to see the whole screen without straining the tendons in his neck; there is in fact no need to move his head at all.

At this moment a man strolls by. A cinema hooligan: noisy looking, snack-heavy, eating popcorn in handfuls and choosing to sit in the middle by the aisle.

You see, this is the problem with sitting at the back. This is the hell you have to go through. He knew he should have stayed where he was. What was he thinking? A man almost in his line of view and munching popcorn! They really shouldn't let you in once the film has begun.

She senses his discomfort even though he tries to hide it.

'It's OK.' She pats him on the knee, and moves to the seat adjacent.

The man in the middle gets up and walks out.

'He's in the wrong screen,' she tells him, still making knee contact. 'It happens all the time.'

They watch the rest of the film, distraction-free, both staying until the very end. Afterwards, in the foyer, he asks her out. A date. To the cinema sometime. And she tells him she doesn't do the cinema coupling thing, or the cinema dating thing. But she will be doing the cinema alone thing next Thursday at 3:30. There's a screening of *Amores Perros* that nobody will want to see around here and it'll be good to see him there, at the back?

And she makes a movement toward him, as if to kiss him, then retreats. And he responds by kissing her. And she kisses him back.

He tells her that it's a date then, and she says no it's not, and he tells her that he'll not be at the 3:30 unless it is a date, and that he's attracted to her and that he doesn't play games.

She kisses him again, and tells him that she doesn't play games either.

Then she leaves.

But she won't go to see *Amores Perros* at the 3:30. And neither will he.

2

Epiphany

Six months ago, Adam had woken with an epiphany: a sudden realisation he hated his friends. Later on that day – the epiphany diluted by tea and coffee and boredom and loneliness and messages of good will from daytime chat shows – he'd thought hate too strong a word and downgraded it to a mixture of dislike and not-having-anything-in-common-with. A re-scaled epiphany, which applied too to work colleagues and others he had difficulty in labelling.

Wandering his flat, he rearranges his things – picking up and putting down a dehydrated plant, a bruised paperback, his only iron, half a candle, a chipped vase, a half box of biscuits.

He does nothing with these objects but give them a cursory glance and return them to their original location. To the impartial observer his actions could seem a little pointless.

Distracted by the biscuits, he rests – sinks into his brown leather sofa and surveys the room.

There were reasons for it, this epiphany. Many. And

that was six months ago. Months of working on his life – writing lists mainly – has led to one obvious course of action, and today he is going to take it.

Opening the box of biscuits, he squints at two pictures on the mantelpiece. Audrey Hepburn looks stunning as usual. Sexy and serene, she peers out into the lounge from her antique picture frame of ornate and tarnished silver, a look that never changes, a poise and strength that soothes him.

Opposite Audrey, on the other side of the mantelpiece, Peter Lorre is in residence (a signed photograph taken on the set of *Casablanca*). The fellow has an altogether different look about him: A Mona Lisa-like quality, with eyes that follow you around the room. An expression too which changes constantly, reflecting Adam's mood.

The biscuits, the peppermint snaps, are milk chocolate, cream-filled, and best consumed warm and soggy (something the box fails to mention). He takes one to the kitchen in search of something to dunk it in.

While making tea and chomping biscuit, he rifles through cupboards: green tea, tinned oranges, corned beef, half packet of Ryvita. Why doesn't he have any stuff? Why throw things away when there's such an obvious use?

The biscuit is consumed quickly, its silver wrapping discarded in a metal pedal bin; fingers are licked and wiped, and the search continues.

Once, there had been too much useless stuff; now he can't find a single knick-knack. He'd been a bit over-enthusiastic on his recent cleaning spree, ridding his apartment of things he didn't care for; any number of them (currently residing at the bottom of the local rubbish tip) would make an ideal present for a woman he doesn't know.

After peering out of the window for several moments,

mumbling occasionally in contemplation, the tea, fully brewed, is ready for consumption.

He takes it to the lounge in search of something to dunk into it.

Until this morning, the plan was not to go – it was to send a message to the group by not going. So he hadn't bought a present. But this morning he'd woken with a greater need for clarity in his life.

His eyes flit towards the mantelpiece and back as the biscuits are eaten in quick succession. A repetitive motion of dunking, looking, and eating, which speeds up as he dismisses the alternatives: like his dehydrated plant, his bruised paperbacks, his only iron, half a candle, a chipped vase, a dwindling box of biscuits; like stopping en route to the party and picking up some champagne and chocolates.

But this evening is too important for chocolates. They're not enough, even for a woman he doesn't know: something more personal is needed.

Picking up Audrey Hepburn, he lets out a short spurt of a sigh. Avoiding eye contact, he turns her over, unfastens the securing flaps and removes the frame's silver backing.

For a full minute he searches for a glossy magazine before remembering they're at the tip, thrown out with the rubbish, the books he'll never read, the clothes he'll not wear, and the bags and bags of knick-knacks.

He uses paper instead – a short stack of clean white A4 paper is placed very carefully to the right of the picture frame. Blowing on the top sheet, he dislodges any dust that may be invisible to the naked eye and places Audrey Hepburn face down on top of it. On top of her he drops a second sheet, pulled from mid stack.

Audrey safe from dust, backing replaced, he looks at the

empty photo frame. It's a great gift. It has some senti-
mental value. It's a one off. And it's expensive.

On the other side of the mantelpiece, lounging in his
less expensive chrome frame, Peter Lorre is smiling at him;
a mood that's now more reflective, and telling Adam he's
being overly generous.

Party

'Yes, he does, he looks like Clive Owen.'

'No, I can't see it.'

'He does. The heartthrob Clive Owen. Look.'

They look at him.

He hates being looked at; studied momentarily, compared to an actor regarded by many as a heartthrob. He hates being compared to anybody. Why can't he be introduced as Adam – you can't make somebody think your friend looks like a movie star, they either think it, or they don't. All this fuss and he's forgotten her name.

Her thought process, though, he remembers; he has seen it before. First, the chicken impression: poke head forward, tense cheeks and eyes, hold, and relax. Then the look, a look he's been waiting for; it follows the in-depth study he's just received – a kind of he's-not-as-attractive-as-Clive-Owen look that starts with hope and excitement and ends in pity, sympathy for not being quite as attractive as some film star. If he had to be compared to anybody, he'd rather it be, say, somebody talented but ugly. He'd rather people say – women say – 'that's ridiculous, he's much better looking'. That's what he wants; what he gets is the look. A look he could have prevented, pre-empted, neutralised. For every positive affirmation, there's a negative to balance it – like telling her he's also been compared to Martina Navratilova. But he can't be bothered: self-deprecation is something else he's given up. (Also, it's been a long time since he's actually been compared to Martina: seventeen years ago his hair was a lighter shade of brown and he wore gold-rimmed glasses over the summer.)

Oh. Never tell that to a woman, (especially before or during sex), that you look like Martina Navratilova – there's always that look of recognition, that she sees the distant similarity, and always at the most inappropriate moment. In any passionate encounter, better off having her think of a heartthrob, or better still, oneself (experience has taught him that, in such an encounter, thinking of female tennis players can be rather a mood killer for your partner).

'No. I still can't see … Wait a minute,' Claire says. 'Who's Clive Owen?'

Claire, that's it, her name is Claire.

'He's the one in *Casino*,' Jay says.

'No,' Adam interjects. '*Croupier*, he was in *Croupier*.'

Jay laughs. 'That's right, he was in *Croupier*,' then under his breath, '*Casino* – what a knob!' and continues: 'You know who he is now? The *Croupier* guy. Oh, and *Gosford Park*. Remember?'

'No.'

'I don't think I look like Clive Owen.' Adam looks for a conclusion to the conversation before they bring passers-by in to give him the look. He does look a bit like him and he knows it – in a certain light, with his hair cut short. It's his liver: a small problem which has given him his dark, deep-set eyes and can make him look moody and a little like Clive Owen. But his hair isn't short, so he's not surprised she doesn't see it, just bothered that he's trapped in this conversation each time Jay introduces him to somebody.

As a child he wondered how minor fashion accessories could transform a person's appearance: how Clark Kent was Superman with glasses and nobody knew. He wondered this until he bought his first pair of glasses and became Martina Navratilova. Without these gold-rimmed spectacles he looked pretty much like Adam King; put them on and he was a whole new person: a tennis superstar.

Since Martina, he has always looked, very superficially, like somebody famous. Never deliberately – he's never cultivated any sort of look; at fifteen, he was Ivan Lendl – weight loss, new glasses, haircut – followed by a host of other tennis players of mixed sex. Then in his twenties things changed, comparisons began to flatter: minor celebrities, pop idols, film stars of varied status, starting with Hugh Grant (floppy hair, contact lenses, a suit like one in a film he never saw, and dimples) and ending with Clive Owen.

'Oh well. He looks like Hugh Grant too,' Jay says, about to run through the list.

Turning to Claire, Adam explains about the hair, the suit, the gold-rimmed glasses, the dimples, the contact lenses, the dark eyes, and then, thinking about his epiphany, realising this is his day of action, and without providing an excuse, he walks off mid-sentence, disappearing into the crowded pub.

First, though, he leaves her a present on the pub table.

He is sure it's not normal, giving presents to complete strangers because they just happen to be dating your friend – but it is expected within the group, and for once he doesn't begrudge it: he'd spent a great deal of time this evening looking for the perfect present, and he gave it willingly.

'You know what,' Claire says to Jay as Adam fades into the crowd, 'he looks a little like you.'

The pub is having an identity crisis: it's trying to be too

many things to too many customers. Multiple themes and attitudes clash: the basement, with its 80s street theme, graffitied walls, pumping music, glossy bar and comfy sofas. The ground floor – the floor he's on – with its spit-and-sawdust, real ale, jukebox and karaoke. And the upper floors with … well, let's just call it erotica (if that's the leather and whip thing).

Queuing for a taxi is an eventful experience. One he looks forward to – a superficially violent atmosphere with an undercurrent of calm.

Later he'll share a taxi with a couple wearing leather hot pants and whip marks. Both will have pink hair, neither will be carrying any cash. An event to savour, except tonight he'll have other things on his mind – like has he been a little too harsh with his friends, or a little too honest.

Adam is aware that he is being watched. Steven, another of his friends, is now looking towards him: while standing over the table of presents, guarding and counting, he occasionally lifts his head in Adam's direction. Steven is the self-proclaimed leader of the group, and responsible for the majority of the events Adam attends. This is Steven's favourite drinking establishment, but one Adam abhors, this floor anyway; he'd rather be somewhere else.

From the middle of the pub, hiding in the crowd, Adam watches the ceremony. The usual present-giving procedure is adhered to. The receiver of the present, Claire, has obviously been well briefed.

Jay stops the queue of late arrivals while Claire passes the present to Steven for inspection. Then Adam's name is ticked off a list.

Once the presents have been opened, the list of presents will be read out publicly.

Conscious of the surveillance, Adam moves deeper into the pub. Avoiding eye contact, he looks towards his shoes – something is stuck to the left one. He bends down and peels it off – a yellow sticky post-it note, which reads '*WATER PLANTS*'.

Straightening up, he finds himself in another familiar conversation:

'So. What you want for your birthday this year?' Steven has found him. It's hardly surprising.

'Nothing. Thanks.'

'Come on. We'll do something big.'

Steven is Adam's oldest friend.

'Of course, it's my birthday soon as well,' Steven continues.

'Yes. I know.'

Steven is the main reason this events culture gets out of hand. And the reason it's worst at this time of year. He expresses a particular interest in Adam's birthday because it's one week after his own. He likes people to believe he's going to get them something special, as a way of encouraging them to buy a bigger present for himself. The more presents he gets, the bigger the present – oh, and the bigger the present cash differential (the cost of the present you bought him, minus the cost of the one he bought you), the happier he is. He thinks of it as respect.

Really Steven would prefer it if we just handed each other wads of cash in brown envelopes like they do in those mafia films he likes.

'No. I'll get you something really nice this year, and a big party?' Steven says, raising his voice with excitement.

Adam starts to run through his honestly-I-don't-want-anything-you-know-I-like-to-be-alone-on-my-birthday routine, then excuses himself; he has to mingle. There is no time for old speeches. Not today. Not on his day of action. He relocates to a quieter corner, by the karaoke platform – it's hardly used, this being more of a jukebox pub.

These events simply consume too much of his energy. Firstly there's the invitation – a telephone call, say, inviting him to an event he doesn't want to go to. Then there's the awkward pause. Then the emotional blackmail: 'Do it for me', 'I'd really appreciate it if you'd come', 'but it's my birthday', all accompanied by the one emotional subtext: don't reject me, you're supposed to be nice to friends. This is where his time goes: birthdays of friends, birthdays of partners of friends, engagements, weddings, christenings. Then there are the new events. Like anniversaries of first dates – they're not celebrated on the actual day, though, that's sacred. No, the event takes place the weekend after the anniversary of a first date (he'd received an invitation in this morning's post). To support a group of ten friends you have to give up at least one entire life. Time and energy he cannot afford.

He spends several minutes in contemplation in his safety position, partly hidden by the large karaoke screen.

People cruise past without noticing. Like Karen. He's been out with her this year on her birthday, and to the birthdays of four now ex-boyfriends. So that's five events.

Filling up with anger, Adam steps up onto a raised karaoke platform at the side of the bar and switches the machine on. This automatically switches off the jukebox and makes him the focus of the room.

'Hello.' He tests the microphone.

'Sing "Hey, hey, we're the Monkees",' a stranger shouts.

'No.' He won't be singing the Monkees.

He takes a breath. Pauses. And takes another breath.

Maybe he should sing something – not the Monkees; Elvis, maybe? He's wondering whether the day-of-action-thing he had embarked on may not be such a good idea, when he becomes aware that he's already started talking:

'As you are all aware. I've … been going through a patch, and, I know it's going to be painful, for all of us, but … um, I never want to see any of you again.'

Silence.

If Adam had in his possession a handkerchief, he would use it now to dab his forehead – a little cliché for the situation, like in those black and white films, but in these situations people do sweat. It's hot. Numerous lights are pointing in his direction, emitting heat, and he would have to confess to being slightly nervous.

He continues: 'No, umm, what I need to say. What I mean to say is, that, I need a break from you all, to sort my life out. And the best way to, umm, fix things is to take a clean break. From you all. Just for six months.'

Public speaking – it's something he could work on during his break. No. No, he'll never follow that up. Besides, he's quite good at this type of thing, normally. He just has to get to the point, say little and leave them wanting more.

What follows is a two-minute well-rehearsed but poorly delivered goodbye speech, followed by a seven-minute babble through cringeland punctuated with silence. Then:

'Any questions?'

The room is silent.

'No? … Well, this is a good-bye then – a double celebration. Ironically, it's my first party with you all, as co-host.' He looks at Claire, the birthday girl, 'If that's OK with you?'

She nods.

'Well, a double celebration. No need to worry if you

haven't brought a present.' His eyes are still fixed on the birthday girl. 'I'm sure Claire will give me a few of hers?'

She nods again.

'Well, then. Goodbye.' He starts to leave the karaoke platform, stops, and says, 'And happy birthday, Claire.'

And the silence is broken: the juke-box blast back in, playing 'Daydream Believer' by The Monkees, and the room returns to normal.

Normal, as if he'd just made a toast to the birthday girl, as if they hadn't heard the rest.

They had, though – Claire had, at least: he sees her sifting through birthday parcels, searching for one to give away, the small pub table in front of her bending now under the weight of presents. Lightening the load, she picks up the two smallest parcels, one in each hand, and tries to work out which is heaviest.

He thinks about it. Thinks maybe he could have picked a more appropriate moment; but every time the group met was inappropriate. It's better to just be quick and direct about these things, he thinks, as if he's doing major life-changing activities like this every week (forgetting it had taken six months of procrastination to gather courage). But for a short moment he is rather proud of himself.

The only other person who appears to have registered what has been said is Mark, who, seemingly happy with the news, greets him with a grin.

'Lucky bastard,' Mark says.

My, my. How very understanding. A reaction he had not expected: the group as a whole don't care, and Mark, a man he's met only three times, is jealous.

'You got your trip planned?'

'Trip?'

'Yeah, where are you off to, Australia? You should go

there, when I went I had a great time.'

'I'm not—'

'Remember my coming home drink, I showed you the photographs. It was fantastic and I only went for two weeks, you're off for six months. Wow.'

'I am not going to Australia.'

'Well you should, or what my friend is the point of a round-the-world air trip? You'll regret it.'

'I'm not doing anything. Not going anywhere, except work and the cinema.' There are things to do, he is sure, he just isn't aware what they are yet; travelling, though, is something he'll not be doing.

'All I'm saying is think about it. Australia. And if you want some suggestions, call me.' Mark pats him on the back and notices his glass of water. 'Now, I'll get you a beer.'

'No, thank ...' But Mark has already joined the bar queue.

Claire, who's been waiting patiently behind Mark, and has made two unsuccessful attempts to interrupt the visit Australia speech, gives Adam a large wide smile and a small rectangular present.

'Why, thank you,' he says, recognising the wrapping paper, 'this really will be useful.'

———

Back home, deflated but still pleased with himself, he sits in his comfy sofa, sipping green tea, holding his present: a kind of leaving present, for years of loyal friendship, given to him by Claire, a woman he'd met this evening.

A slow muffled thudding noise seeps through the wall from a neighbour's flat – he pays it no attention.

He unwraps the present – the chrome picture frame –

slides out its glass and returns Peter Lorre to his usual position: on the mantelpiece with Audrey. Now that's a film he would like to have seen.

3

Leopards and Spots

The problem – one of them – with friends is they assume you're the same as when they met you. It's that old first impressions cliché. If, for instance, you drank a lot, or ate a lot, didn't know much about music, couldn't spell certain words, or whatever, in the formative years of your friendship, it's expected that you will remain that same person forever: that you'll always want to drink large quantities of alcohol; that you could never start liking popular music, or reading novels. (Even if you haven't had a drink in two years. Even if it's for medical reasons.)

The problem is compounded when your colleagues, friends and family – let's collectively call them people – religiously believe a second cliché: a leopard never changes its spots.

Adam doesn't know whether that is true or not. But he does know that leopards don't celebrate birthdays, or anniversaries. He's not sure whether they even hunt in packs, leopards, let alone spend time together. No. Leopards keep to themselves. They like to be on their own.

The Colour Purple

He's bored – he always is on a Sunday whether there's an event to go to or not. He hates the weekend, hated it when he had friends, hates it now he doesn't. The reasons have changed. The emotion's the same.

From the lounge, he wanders around the flat, room to room, with no real purpose, ending up in the kitchen, making another cup of tea. Opening the cupboards, he searches for inspiration, anything of interest – some forgotten-about high-calorie food that may keep at least his digestive system busy for a couple of hours. There's little food here, nothing he'd not seen ten minutes ago – he'd cleared the cupboard too of food he had no intention of eating. He thinks about frying some corned beef, eating it with Ryvita crispbread: time for a re-stock, he thinks – not today, though: soon.

Returning to the lounge, he looks at the television and covers it with a piece of green silk fabric that was lying on the floor. He sits for five minutes staring at it, sipping his tea and reflecting. Strange he's never bored in the week: he never has these fits of boredom when he takes a day off work. He'd be quite happy with fried corned beef in Ryvita if it were Monday. Now, though, at least he has a reason to be bored: he has less to do, less to occupy him – now his brain is freed from dreading the next social ordeal. Right now he could be at – he looks at his diary – Terry and Samantha's 'One Year Until We're Getting Married' barbecue, a sort of engagement party sequel.

With a large black marker-pen he creates more space in his life, flicking through this week's itinerary, wiping days out in bold black swipes. Wiping out Saturday (Samantha's barbecue), and Sunday (Steven's birthday), and Monday (reminder to buy a moving house gift – for whom, he cannot recall), he makes more room, more time to do stuff. On a high, he continues through the next month, deleting more from his life: birthdays, anniversaries, wedding suit fittings, a wedding reception, another birthday. Making more time, creating more space.

After wiping out the rest of the calendar year, he stops, drops the diary in the bin, and returns to his new hobby: staring at the green fabric covering the TV set.

He wonders what he'll do with his spare time: no doubt something he'd actually enjoy, like … like … thinking about what he wants to do. Staring at the green fabric is fine, but hardly a substantial enough activity to fill all the room he's just freed up. His big plan so far has been to create space in his life, and the only filler he's thought about is more time at the cinema.

The thought occurs to him while staring at the fabric, that he may have been overly ambitious discarding both television and friendship in the same month. His reasoning had been sound – that since they were the only two things he did with his time there was a distinct danger that by stopping one activity the other would expand to fill the void: television and a lack of willpower could sap his new-found freedom.

He'd been without television for two weeks so far. The initial separation had been easy – throwing a piece of fabric over the set and pretend it's not there – and had worked too, for three hours, until he'd realised he was missing *Seinfeld*. And then watching television that night became all too easy. Without thinking, he'd yanked off the fabric and hit the on button.

Seinfeld, a sitcom lasting half an hour, had started at midnight, and he'd switched off the television at three in the morning – it was as if he'd had to stay up and catch up on the three hours of television he'd missed. (He also turned up three hours late for work the next day – his whole life had been displaced. He'd got television-lag and had to leave work early that day to recover.) Worse than that, he'd been introduced to a programme called *Late Night Poker*, which unsurprisingly starts late and coincides with his coming home from an over-demanding social life.

And it's not those programmes he has a problem with watching: it's an enjoyable experience watching *Seinfeld* and *Late Night Poker*. It's the stuff in between that's the problem, the stuff that requires willpower to stop watching.

Eventually, his strategy for television avoidance had worked. With a little tinkering, and a lot more obstacles, he has managed to limit himself to watching television only twice in the last two weeks.

Today, he stares at the fabric knowing that watching American sitcoms is a harder task. The initial barrier, the green silk fabric, is still an obstacle. OK, it's not much of one, not camouflage, not a good what-do-you-call-it, a disguise, but if he yanks off the fabric now, or if it falls off (which it constantly does), he'll still not see the screen. There is a second obstacle: yellow sticky post-it notes swamp the screen. He'd have to peel them off. Which takes longer than you think, because there's a ritual which he adheres to: he has to peel off the notes, read what's written on every third one and place them in a neat pile on the arm of the sofa.

Removing the fabric and the yellow post-it notes, he'd

be able to see the screen, only the television wouldn't work: it's not plugged in. He'd have to move it across the room, so the lead can reach the socket. First he'd have to move the cabinet blocking the socket holes, and he'd have to move the items from the top of the cabinet because otherwise they'd slide off like last time and that's just unfair to Charlie. (His goldfish.)

A phone call interrupts his boredom.

He lets it ring. And ring. It stops ringing before the answer machine cuts in. Then starts again. He thinks about unplugging the thing, then:

'Hello.' He answers it.

'Hi. What colour's fashionable this summer?' the voice says. The owner of the voice, Steven, had asked him this before, two days ago.

'I don't know. You asked me that two days ago.'

'No. I asked you that a year ago.'

He had been asked that one year ago, true, and two days ago, and two years ago, and countless other years ago. He'd been deliberating putting this on 'the list', but this isn't just a negative characteristic, it's fundamentally Steven. And the list is irrelevant now they're taking a SIX MONTH break.

'I've got some white jeans I need to die, and was just wondering if you knew what's the best colour for this summer.'

'No.'

The fact that Steven is asking such a question shows how little he knows about Adam. That is already on the list. Steven asks him to think about it, and Adam tells him he won't, and Steven says they'll talk about it later.

'No, we won't talk about it later. Did you hear my speech yesterday?'

He knows Steven did. Steven was sitting at the table of

gifts, next to the birthday girl, what's-her-name, Claire.

'You're an awful orator, aren't you. I almost wet myself.'

He will not be sidetracked, and can't recollect any laughing.

'So why are you calling me to talk fashion? Something I know nothing about?'

'Yes. I know. Where did you get that top you wore yesterday?'

You would think, if this conversation had been with anybody else, that they had been hurt by what was said yesterday and wanted to let off steam. But no, this is a typical conversation with Steven. At thirty Adam feels at least twenty years too old for this kind of discussion.

'Let me make this clear, Steven. I'm taking a break from my old life, and that means no communication with the old crowd for six months at least, maybe forever. No birthdays. No weddings. No anniversaries. No Leaving drinks. No contact.'

'OK, but you're still coming out on Sunday week.'

'No.'

'But ... but ... but ... it's my birthday.'

If Adam tried here, if he really tried, he could make Steven cry. Or he could give in one last time and celebrate a birthday (at least it's somebody he knows). Or he could stick to his plan.

'I'm sorry,' Adam says, but Steven has already hung up.

Adam had managed, with a great deal of effort, to amass around him a group of very similar personalities. The group, his friends, were all disparaging in the same way as Steven: undermining with negative little snipes, aiming at funny and hitting irritation. Individually they were a nuisance; combined, they zapped energy. Jay was the only exception. Adam really may send for him once his new life is established. Jay is borderline on Adam's list: his personality deficit had only just reached twenty.

Adam attempts to return to his boredom, but it's gone, kicked out by anger; he switches his phone off for the rest of the day.

4

The Lobby

In the lobby, in his office building, he waits for the lift and is joined by a man: it's enough to make you take the stairs. Consider it anyway. The man has a vague, marketing quality about him, and a smile indicating they've made conversation at least once over the last three years. Adam looks at his shoes – no yellow post-it notes today – and keeps his thoughts to himself.

It's a danger area for him, the lift, like the photocopier, his work's kitchen and the canteen. Anywhere, in fact, he might be trapped in a queue-forming situation. They say the English aren't communicative, and they're right: in the street, in the shopping hall, on the bus. You may take the same journey to work every day, see the same person and not say a word, not know his name. If your journey is an hour, say, and you see him in both directions, to and from work, you'd be in his company for ten hours a week. Ten hours every week. More time than you spend with a best friend, no doubt – if, that is, you're one of those people who has friends (and that's up to you, he'll not judge you for it).

This doesn't apply to Adam directly, of course, because he doesn't take the bus. He walks. And it only takes him thirty minutes. And he never walks with the same people. He sees the same people some of the time, like the guy who owns the fruit shop, but he only stops if he's run out of bananas, and that's a rare occurrence, and he doesn't know his name. And people are on the whole friendlier here than most places. So the thought he was having could apply if he worked elsewhere – London, say: one of the few advantages to the place is being ignored. Why can't we all just live up to our stereotype and leave each other alone? This just will not do.

Anyway, what's going on? The point is this: if a fictitious man can sit next to a fictitious stranger for ten hours a week and not exchange pleasantries, the strangers he meets at work could have the common decency not to talk to him at every available opportunity!

A glance left: marketing man is still there, displaying indications of impending communication. What right has he? Just because they share the same employer? Nonsense: it does not make sense.

'Hi,' says Marketing Man. A common opening line.

Adam: a nod.

'Do anything last night?'

Adam again looks at his shoes; a silence long enough to convey he doesn't want to talk; a little shake of the head; then:

'No. Nothing.'

And he's left alone. They step into the lift, side-by-side, facing forwards, not talking, following the laws of non-communication. Marketing Man presses the door-close button frequently, trying to speed the journey along. Adam continues to check for signs of stray post-it notes. All is well. A struggling silence, but for the best. Until floor one.

'So you didn't do anything last night?'

'No.'

'Watch anything good?'

'No.' He hadn't watched any television, and he's not going to talk about watching green fabric, even though he's starting to enjoy the experience – after the first hour it has a mesmerising yet relaxing quality, meditation-like, he imagines. Telling anybody about it would be doing them a kindness, but it's not socially acceptable, and it'll send out the wrong message. People like sticking to what they know.

He's wary of conversations like this. It's how friendships start: a casual meeting in the lobby, a common liking for doing certain things, and that's it – a friend.

They exit the lift side by side, separate, and walk off in opposite directions.

The attack continues in his work's kitchen.

'Having a good day?' somebody asks.

Really – if he's in need of a friend he'll join an agency.

'YES,' he says, dropping a banana skin into a bin and leaving the vicinity before things turn nasty, 'thank you.'

First, somebody wants to know how you're feeling, or what you saw on television last night. Next, they're wanting you to come to their birthday, be Godfather to their child, eat with them at weekends. A thoroughly draining experience he does not want to have. He has no storage space for friends in this new life, no room for new ones while the old ones clog up his phone line.

The Café

Adam's had a long conversation with his boss about nothing, and is eating his breakfast at his desk when the phone rings. He deliberates about answering before picking it up.

'Hello'

'Hi, Adam?'

He recognises the voice. 'How did you get my number?'

No reply.

He hadn't asked her name, the chocolate crunch woman. And she hadn't asked his name either. They hadn't swapped names or numbers, only saliva.

'How do you know my name?'

A pause: short and accompanied by a muffled giggle.

'What's your name?'

'Yvette'

'No, it's not.'

'Eve.'

'No.'

Adam is deeply cautious of any woman who introduces herself as anything that can be shortened to Eve. He knows there are people called Eve, Yvette and Yvonne out there, but being named Adam, and through experience, he has built a healthy suspicion: usually a woman introducing herself as Eve was being childish, predictable and not at all funny.

'My name's Mada.'

'No that's Adam backwards!'

'Maddie?'

'I told you I don't play games,' he says.

'I don't play games,' she replies in a deep, playful voice.

Quickly, on the pad beside his phone, he scribbles a note:

Lattee Woman: Childish

'How many *ees* in latte?' he asks.

'One.'

He tears out the sheet of paper, bins it and starts afresh:

Latte Woman: Childish.

'We need to meet.'

'Why?'

'It's too important to talk about over the telephone. Let's meet for lunch, I'm right outside your office now.'

'Oh.' He doesn't bother asking how she knows where he works – there have been too many awkward pauses in their relationship already. He lets it slide.

'It's nine o'clock,' he says, peering out of the window at a phone box. He sees nobody, wonders if she's using a mobile, or another phone box, and scans the rest of the street.

'I know it's nine o'clock,' she says. 'Let's meet for lunch at lunchtime.'

'OK.'

She tells him to meet her in a café at one. A patisserie, she calls it. Opposite the side entrance of his office and along two shops to the left he'll find an alleyway; that's where the entrance is, though the café does have a window with views of both the side street and his building.

Then she hangs up.

He again peeks out onto the street. His office faces onto

the main road. By standing on a chair in the far right-hand corner and hanging onto the blinds (it's a swivel chair, and he completes a three-sixty degree turn before realising the need for support), he is able to see part of the road to which she referred. But he can't see the alleyway, or the café window – which he imagines her to be standing at now.

Valuable seconds he wastes, face squished against glass, unsuccessfully attempting to see more of the street. It's of no use, the windows don't open; if they did, he could, he's sure, see the café which she had mentioned.

Holding onto the blinds, carefully he steps down from the swivel chair.

At his desk he paces.

Vantage points of use: the roof, the Women's toilet (the windows open – well, they do in the Men's, so he'll keep to that assumption), and his boss's office (the only office with a view of that street).

By the time he got to the roof she'd be gone. His boss's office is nearer but the man's simply too stressful.

He sets off to the Women's toilet and gives up his quest en route: she's bound to be gone already, she's hardly going to sit in a café all morning waiting for him.

He wonders how she knows so much about him, thinks about whether she's been following him. He often thinks he's being followed but is always mistaken. An over-active imagination has landed him in trouble on countless occasions. Never has he been afraid to turn to a stranger and ask, 'Why are you following me?' You see how he builds his collection – embarrassing moments, dirty looks, phone numbers too. (It's how he met his ex-friend Karen. Do you remember – the seductress? Was she introduced? Four boyfriends, four boyfriends' birthdays, and a party of her own – you remember now? No. Never mind.)

He leaves the office by the side entrance at twelve fifty-five and immediately spots the alleyway and the window to which she referred as he crosses the street. He peers in on his approach: a rather dainty cafe, clean and welcoming, glass counters, rustic tables and marble flooring.

He scans the tables – she's not there yet. His watch reads twelve fifty-nine.

How mad could she be if she knows about an environment like this, he wonders; it's nice, the serenity of the café – so close to his office and he never noticed.

The café is busy, though there are still tables available.

He sits at a table next to the window, then immediately relocates, moving far enough away to be sitting in an area of shade while keeping in peripheral vision both window and entrance.

It's a most quiet café considering the number of customers. He'd expected the volume to be much louder from the outside, when he'd looked in through the window. There's something odd about it. The people too. Strange to have such an eclectic mix: no particular type, nothing observable in common – except, perhaps, an absence of chatter.

He glances at his watch. And he waits …

'Hi, Adam.'

She appears from behind him, touching his hair then shoulder, gesturing there's no need to get up – a thought that hadn't crossed his mind. She had crept up on him without using the entrance; there was only one way in, and she had not used it.

She sits opposite him and beckons a waiter over.

'Hello ...' – he's not sure what to call her.

'... Yvette,' she prompts.

An awkward silence while Adam rearranges the table, moving a vase from one side to the other in an attempt to hide his fluster over the naming issue.

'You like the flowers?' she says.

He hadn't thought about them one way or the other.

Another silence while he thinks about them – he'll not just say yes for the convenience of it. He looks at the flowers, smells them, thinks, then says, 'Yes.'

'Thank you,' she says, as if he'd given a compliment.

This bothers him: her weirdness, and that she knows too much about him.

'You have ID on you?'

She *umms* and *ahhs* while laying a small black bag on the table and rifling through it. A full minute later she zips it up. 'No, I ain't got no proof,' she says in an accent that's not her own but has a familiarity about it, as if she's trying to impersonate somebody he's only vaguely acquainted with.

He points to the bag.

'Mind if I?'

'No.' She moves the vase and pushes the bag towards him.

He unzips the bag – it's empty.

'Nice, isn't it; I just bought it.'

Appearing in cafés without using entrances, looking through empty bags for invisible contents, knowing everything about him – his name, where he works, his work phone number (she'd called him on the direct line and bypassed the switchboard) – this, he thinks, is most abnormal; yet arouses him.

How much about him exactly does she know: His shoe

size? The names of his friends? His neighbours? Why he hates …

'Why do I hate Bovril?'

She appears not to comprehend.

'The drink, Bovril – why do I hate it?'

She shrugs an I-don't-know.

OK then. He feels a little silly. And hates Bovril because an uncle told him it was made from crushed-up worms (and though he's known this not to be true for the last twenty-five years, he still can't even bear to look at a jar).

'Bovril? I don't know,' she says, 'but I hate it too.'

'Ahh. And why is that?'

'I just do.'

He nods an acknowledgement.

So she doesn't know everything. And it is quite possible that there are good reasons for the things she does know about him, several good reasons or coincidences. Reasons, too, why she's not carrying ID.

'Hope you can prove a name like that. I'd like to see some real proof of identity next time we meet,' he says, thinking ahead to their non-date on Thursday week. 'Until then I shall call you Latte.'

'Fine,' she says, smiling, 'and I'll call you Adam.'

A waiter arrives and asks for their order.

'I'll have a cappuccino. And—' nodding at Latte – 'Latte?'

'I'll have a latte,' says Latte.

The waiter recaps, looking at his notepad: 'So two lattes and one cappuccino.' Adam replies: 'No that's just one latte, and one cappuccino, thank you!'

Immediately he sees the hole in his naming plan.

The waiter stands for a moment, confused. Latte gives him a little nod, and he continues.

'So,' he says, scrubbing out his notes and smiling at Latte, 'that's one cappuccino for the gentleman and a latte for Yvette.' Latte nods again and the waiter leaves.

Of course anybody could say they were Yvette and introduce themselves to the waiter by that name.

He's felt embarrassment before over this naming issue, from the other side: he'd been at a party and a woman had introduced herself to him as Eve, shortened from Yvonne, and he'd introduced himself as Adam, and she didn't believe him – she just made fun of him all night.

An elderly couple sitting at the next table look over. The gentleman winks at Latte, says hello, calls her Yvette and asks who her man friend is. The piece of social banter which follows lets Adam know, with ninety-nine percent certainty, that she is who she says she is.

'I own the coffee shop,' she tells him. 'It's a family business.'

'Oh,' he says. Another embarrassing moment for his collection. Except he's not actually embarrassed, just aware that he should be. After all, she's the one who's been prying into his life; he'll stick to being suspicious.

The waiter brings them their coffees, plonks them on the table: one cappuccino with a proper fluffy topping – and real, grated dark chocolate – and one latte with … he sniffs – cinnamon and fresh raspberries. And he'd thought the coffee at the cinema to be stylish because it came with Flakes and chocolate crunch!

On the napkin lying beside his cappuccino, in a fancy French font, is the name of the café: *Yvette's*. The name, he remembers now, was also above the door when he entered. She tells him that it's been here for twenty years, the café, and it's always been called *Yvette's* – her parents named it after their only daughter. And no, she wasn't French, and no, neither were her parents; but their first date was to the cinema, to see a French film, and the leading actress was called Yvette. She tells him that she's told this story so many times she's thought about having it embossed on the napkins. And that she hasn't because she quite likes telling the story.

A pause. She sips her latte and lets out a low, rumbling '*Mmmm*'.

He is envious; he is more than happy with his real grated chocolate cappuccino but the thought of a real raspberry topping makes his mouth water.

'How's your cappuccino?' she says, pronouncing the word properly, like an Italian.

He sips. He sighs.

'Nice.' He feels relaxed. 'The chocolate is very well suspended,' he adds, wishing he'd said something more interesting; suddenly becoming aware of her sex.

'Good. I knew you'd get it. Appreciate it.'

She tells him that she sees him go to work every day; sees him while she's polishing the patisserie window and writing the morning menu – he stops at the crossing on the corner by his office building waiting for the lights to change. She notices him there, at the end of the road, always at the same time, at exactly five to nine, sometimes eating a banana, sometimes just carrying one, like this morning.

He had no idea he was this punctual. This predictable. In fact he likes to think of himself as somebody who isn't predictable at all. He leaves for work at the same time every morning, but he takes different routes each day to spice things up a little – he pretends he's going to work somewhere else. He does, though, always use that crossing at the end of the street.

He says nothing, but thinks about them lying in bed together. He's certainly not going to mention Martina Navratilova. *DO NOT MENTION MARTINA.*

She also sees him at the cinema, on Thursday afternoons. Every Thursday afternoon at Screen Seven, even if they keep the same film rolling, so she knows he's seen *Amores Perros* twice, at least, and that he's seen *Run Lola Run* twice and *Roseanna's Grave* twice, along with a number of other films, other titles which she reels off. Oh, and she tells him she sees him in his office too, every morning at nine o'clock.

He does not tell her that it is his boss's office she sees him in, that his office cannot be observed from the café, and he does not tell her about Martina Navratilova, why would he?

Of course she may not want to sleep with him. He's hopeless at seeing stuff like that. Even though she knows everything about him – where he works, what he does on Thursday afternoons, his name, his work phone number – he couldn't be sure; it doesn't imply any kind of attraction to him, just knowledge.

There's a spoon, hidden underneath the edge of his saucer. Adam holds it lightly between his fingers, uses it to pat the foam of his cappuccino.

'How can you suspend raspberries on a latte? How do you get the suspension?' he says. 'I mean, I can see how it'd work with a cappuccino.'

This is where he'd like to be Clive Owen. Would he have made a lame comment about coffee? – no, he'd be assured and sexually aggressive. This is also where friends came in handy: telling him stuff like that. Karen (his ex-friend) had once spelt 'she fancies you' in magnetic letters on his fridge; said he should assume it to be true in all cases, and knew of no occasion on which it had not been. He feels a pang of sadness at leaving them, those friends, who'd tell him the obvious.

The right thing had been done: two days on, he's had two days of peace and time to do what he wants. Normally he'd be present-hunting now, instead he's having lunch with an attractive woman and sipping the best cappuccino he's ever tasted.

He spends ten minutes listening to Yvette talking about coffee and cake and watching for flirtations: playing with her hair, passing raspberries into his mouth, giving him her phone number, the obvious signs on his I'm-interested-in-you list.

He finishes his coffee, scraping the bottom of the white cup with his spoon; noting the time – two o'clock, he's late for an important meeting – he asks the waiter for the bill, but Yvette tells him it's on the house.

Getting up to leave, he remembers there had been a point to the meeting; he stops, and sits back down.

'What was so important?' he asks. 'What was the purpose of this meeting?'

'Yes,' she says. 'It's too important to talk about now. We need more time.'

First Impressions

The meeting room is bright, light and spacious; white walls, chrome furnishings, a Perspex partition with a view of the office, a large window with a view of the café, and an agitated boss who's been waiting three minutes as Adam arrives.

Adam catches the small pink notepad frisbee thrown at him as he enters.

'Go on, have a guess,' his boss says, 'how much this cost.'

He'd rather not 'have a go' as it's put recently, seemingly at the start of every meeting.

'Have a go.' The Boss laughs, 'Never guess.'

He thinks about saying nothing. Just standing there and counting the number of times he hears that phrase. But as the meeting is somewhat short – half an hour – and as he's already had one meeting today he couldn't see the point of, and—

'How much, have a go. Come on. Take a guess.'

—and as this is his boss – don't ask him how – and is clearly expecting some kind of answer—

'You'll never guess.'

'OK. OK. OK.'

—he'll have to guess.

'I'll guess.'

He rubs his hands together in thought: it's cheap, it always is, and the last time, this morning, his guess was too high – a Parker pen he'd guessed cost two pounds (a sale price) had been bought for eighty pence. A notepad like this, small but expensive, looks like it's worth six pounds, so:

'Three pounds?'

'No …' Wildly, The Boss shakes his head.

'You got it for free. Zero pence.' He pre-empts any try-again comeback.

The Boss hackles in an over-exaggerated, head-thrown-back, fiendish, arch-criminal way he's copied from a film he's seen.

'No.'

Adam turns the notepad over. The bottom reveals a price tag of nine pounds.

'That's expensive,' he says, falling into the trap.

'I know. It's Michael's – what a knobber.'

Noticing somebody else has arrived back late from lunch, The Boss leaves: meeting over.

Half the time he spends with The Boss he zones out into semi-consciousness, where he can think of more important issues; or he'll count, swear-words or random phrases, or both: he'll finish a meeting and that's all he'll remember – a series of numbers. On this occasion, though, believing there was something worth talking about, and being faced with a direct question that required an answer (it's a rare occurrence), he'd fallen into the trap of actually listening to what The Boss was saying. This information is now stored in Adam's lobes. No matter what he does, a storage compartment in the brain will keep hold of this information: he'll remember that Michael Cummings paid nine pounds for a notepad.

He's a good mind to charge The Boss rent: a fee every time his brain recalls that fact. It's pollution of the worst kind: mind garbage dumped without permission.

An article he'd read recently claimed that every time you see somebody your subconscious re-lives every experience you've ever had with them. As long as he sees The Boss, he'll smell garbage.

Sitting at The Boss's desk, looking through the partition, Adam watches the notepad being passed around the office, person to person, The Boss's head continually engaged in a wild sideways shake as he outwits his employees.

Don't be fooled by this first impression. The Boss can put on a happy face when he wants too. He comes across as irritating but harmless. But he's not; this is as nice as he gets – he's not always this charming, even with him.

Adam peers through the window onto the street, towards the café, listening to random guess-how-much numbers being shouted out in the background. An elderly couple sit in the café window, laughing and sipping cappuccino. The elderly woman glances around, then dabs her partner's nose with a spoonful of froth.

There have been no swear-words today, so far, unless you count 'knobber', and he doesn't: it wasn't said with the same passion as the regular swearing. Is that a positive? Yes, it's a positive.

Of course, it will pass, this phase The Boss is going through. Soon The Boss will revert to his usual nature; he's one leopard who invariably does follow that cliché.

Adam is still looking at the couple in the café when normality returns – he is disturbed by the noise of several loud expletives originating from behind him. Somebody obviously knows Michael Cummings a little too well.

The Boss snaps the notepad from the hand of a cleaner and stomps back towards his office.

The door is firmly shut.

'F**KING C**T,' he says to nobody.

'You still here?' he says to Adam.

So you see, first impressions aren't quite what they seem.

What follows can only be described as a more normal meeting; if 'meeting' is the right word.

Afterwards, Adam sits at his desk and updates a spreadsheet: swear count totals from the meeting. The graph shows a definite decline in the use of the word SH*T over the last two weeks, but C*NTS have risen by over thirty percent.

Thinking

'You can't suddenly decide you don't need friends. It's not like, say, shoes ... Oh fuck, not shoes ... err ... I mean not like ... Umm ... Well, I need everything, don't I, or I wouldn't have it, would I? So you can't just decide you don't need friends because you do. Everybody does.'

There are eight other messages on his answer machine: seven from Steven seeking adulation and fashion advice and one from Mark wishing him good luck on his trip, and making sure he has the correct mailing address for any postcards Adam may send on his travels.

Sitting in his comfortable sofa, sipping green tea (there are no biscuits available to dunk), he looks at the green fabric hanging over the television and thinks about Yvette. He's trying to lose friends at the moment, not gain them. But he's allowed to gain a lover, isn't he? In this new life he's inventing. Yes, he's allowed a lover.

He thinks about her body-language at their meeting, the little details he'd ticked on his she's-interested-in-you list. He starts doubting them.

Had she played with his food? Yes. Had she played with her hair? Yes. Or had she just been wiping the food from her hair? – he had sprayed her, laughing inappropriately, and with a mouth full of chocolate cappuccino – in which event, had it been more a case of personal grooming than flirtation? He is undecided.

He thinks through the other things on his list. There are obvious and plausible reasons for all of them. Yes, she had given him her phone number, written it on a napkin and pushed it across the table at him. But she may need contact for some other reason. There was, after all, that important thing she wanted to discuss – the reason for their meeting. He is still undecided.

A slow thudding noise penetrates a wall of his flat – he pays it no notice.

THUD.

The noise is interspersed with his neighbour shouting slogans, the louder ones are clearly audible.

THUD.

'And you're outta here.'

Adam, deep in thought, is staring intensely at the green fabric when it falls off the television set. He's hit with a blinding flash of yellow post-it notes.

'Must be sexually assertive', 'She fancies you', 'Buy more shoes', 'Eat more roughage'. Most of the notes on his TV screen encourage him not to watch television: *'Don't watch me', 'NO TV', 'TV makes you stupid'*, lame phrases like that, only he found he never looked at them so he mixed them with positive thoughts and affirmation, things he'd find useful. His ex-friend Karen had also added some slogans – the ones that are jumping up and grabbing his attention now.

He re-covers the television. Not watching it has given him a more acute sense of hearing: he is able to hear other people's televisions over huge distances. This ability to hear television now borders superhero. Right now, he knows that High-Pitched Squeak Man (a neighbour) is watching *Frasier*, as is a man in the ground floor flat (Adam lives on floor two), and he knows Sockball (his other neighbour, who has just finished making thudding noises) has switched the *News* on. Listening very quietly, while holding his breath, he can just make out some *Frasier* dialogue. He recognises the episode and lets out a long laugh in time with the punch-line, then stops – he's thinking of the wrong episode. But this one's equally as good, better in fact, an episode he's only partly seen (he'd caught the opening before heading out to a birthday party and it's always bothered him that he missed the ending).

There isn't enough time to plug the television in – he checks his watch: the show finishes at ten thirty. Adam attempts to boost the sound by opening the door and the window. This works too, briefly – his head sticking out of the window, one ear pointing to the ground floor flat, the other towards his neighbour – until it rains. And that's it. No more sitcom.

Towel-drying his hair, a thought crosses his mind – about Yvette and her urgent news: that there isn't any. That Yvette just wants to see him. That she's not a lunatic. That there are obvious and believable reasons behind her actions, and … that she does find him attractive. After all, they had kissed, exchanged saliva – a fact he'd recalled with his head out of the window. Oh, and they have a date too, to the cinema, Screen Seven, to see *Amores Perros* at 3:30.

He relaxes: if there was some news relevant to him, and if it was urgent, she'd have told him already.

5

The Thing

He stops at the lights and looks down the side street. The menu is out and Yvette is cleaning the window. They simultaneously notice and wave at each other.

He checks his watch – it's five to nine – and decides to skip work for a long fifteen minutes so they can have croissants and coffee, which this time he will insist on paying for; and he can confront her on this important, and non-existent, thing she keeps referring to.

'They're closing the programme,' she tells him.

'What programme?' he asks, sipping a double choc cappuccino with fresh raspberries.

'They're closing the programme at the cinema. They're only going to show mainstream films.'

'Oh,' he says.

'Oh?' she says. 'That all you can say? I thought you'd be upset. I thought you'd understand.'

'I am,' he says, though he'd been distracted from emotional negativity by coffee: the redness of the raspberry and the darkness of the chocolate affect him on so many levels: vision, taste, that sense of satisfaction he has when he gets something he really wants. He'll be genuinely upset when he gets to work and the coffee's instant, but he'll have to fake it for now.

'I am,' he repeats.

He'll have to pull himself together. There's a genuine problem here, and somebody to solve it with.

The raspberries aren't whole, they've been chopped – big enough so you can still see the individual sections, small enough to prevent sinking.

He drinks the cappuccino quickly to get rid of the distraction.

'Maybe we could get enough people. They may kick up a fuss. Ask them why they're not screening it.'

'That's an idea … we could think about,' she says.

She hates it, she tells him through her eyes and her posture.

'I'm just thinking off the top of my head here. What do you call it, free thinking, that Virginia Woolf thing.'

'Stream of conscious.'

Another pause.

'That's it. Stream of conscious.'

It's not a bad idea is it, really – especially for nine o'clock in the morning, especially before breakfast, not a totally awful idea – just not a great one. Could be better, a little more realistic. But the tone has gone sour, and after another raspberry and chocolate cappuccino drunk in silence, he leaves and makes his way to work.

Arriving in the office at nine twenty-three, his boss calls him in for a meeting. From The Boss's body posture he guesses this will not be a guess-how-much conversation.

He tells Adam to sit.

Adam sits.

Then he zones out and thinks of Yvette. Yesterday he made the rare mistake of actually listening to the man, properly, and isn't going to make that mistake again. Mind garbage is another thing he is getting rid of. He's quite good at multi-tasking when he needs to be. He lets his subconscious deal with whatever The Boss is talking about and frees part of his mental energy, his conscious thought, to work on the altogether more important problem of saving Screen Seven.

After several minutes and nothing to show for it, he senses The Boss is drawing to the end of his conversation and tunes back in.

'And don't let the C**TS rip you off.'

'I certainly will not.'

'You make that deal … And remember, you need any help, I'll come along and talk to the SH**S. I'll give them a right slap.'

He remembers the last time The Boss accompanied him to 'close a deal': the suppliers increased their prices by thirty percent and they had been lucky to get any parts at all. Adam had been left little room to negotiate – spending the rest of the afternoon, as he did, persuading them not to call the police.

It's an incident The Boss also remembers.

Eating his banana at his desk, he fills with disappointment. The only thing he's planned in this new life of his is more trips to the cinema, seeing cinema outside work hours now his evenings are his own. He was going to see everything, but still the thing he looks forward to the most is the Screen Seven Thursday matinee. Apart from the tranquillity, the feeling he gets from thinking he's alone in that screen, there's now the additional significance of its providing continuity in his life.

By the end of his banana he's worked up: there will be no films from Spike Lee, no David Lynch, and no Italian Classic season, which means no Nanni Moretti, not even his latest – the winner of best film at Cannes and it'll still not screened. The Coen Brothers would face the axe too. How could they not show the Coen Brothers? They're not even subtitled.

Also there'll be no French Canadian films. He sighs. Then remembers he's never seen a French Canadian film at Screen Seven. He's seen them in London. Two of them, both directed by Robert Lepage. One called *Le Polygraphe* at the ICA; the other, *Le Confessionnal,* at the National Film Theatre. Both times, on the way home he'd been stuck on the train for three hours.

For the rest of the day, and for the next couple of days, film titles will pop randomly into his head. Films that were going to be shown in Screen Seven but now look doubtful. Films like *Monsoon Wedding, Timecode, Chuck and Buck, Following,* the next Woody Allen film, the next great French Film.

He'll wonder if they'll spare the French, given a large enough advertising budget – he knows some people went to see the film *Amélie,* though he personally didn't notice anybody, in Screen Seven.

The Following

Something is missing. Hate? Irritation? Stress? Dread? Whatever it is, he finds it disconcerting. He checks his answer machine. Nothing. He has no new messages.

Looking towards the wall socket he notices the machine and phone are not plugged in. He plugs them in.

They start to ring.

He unplugs them.

How did it come to this? He was always the last in the group to dislike anybody, whatever group he was part of – at school, at work (he'd even liked his boss, his directness) – he's always been the last to see why somebody was irritating and the first to find the good in a man. Sitting now blissfully alone in his flat, he tries to think of the reason for this particular change in his personality, a single event maybe that triggered in him the need to be on his own, but can't.

Sinking back into his comfortable sofa, he sips his green tea and watches the green fabric hanging over the television set. A noise seeps through the wall from his neighbour's flat: through brick and plasterboard and white paint.

THUD.

It's getting louder by the day, yet still he pays it little attention.

In his conversation with Yvette he had been useless. He'd been useless over this whole matter. Not very instructive or useful. A drain on coffee stock. He wants to *say* something next time, come up with a plan. Yes, that would impress. A day-saving plan.

His neighbour on the other side, High-Pitched Squeak Man, is watching a home improvement programme with an instantly recognisable theme tune. The tune today has a tinny-echo quality to it, as if it's being watched in the bathroom.

In the kitchen he rifles through cupboards searching in vain for something to dunk in his tea, but finds nothing. There's hardly any food here. Certainly nothing that could be dunked into a cup of green tea, even with his imagination.

Leaving the flat, he walks towards the corner shop thinking up a plan.

He can see why Yvette is sceptical. Just because people sign a petition doesn't mean they'll actually turn up. How true. And if they do, if the programme is saved, will they turn up a second time?

Adam likes to pace – it's where his best ideas come from. Like streamlining his life. Before his big epiphany, the night before, he'd been out for a long walk and had thought of nothing in particular. And in the morning he'd woken with a rather large and sudden realisation.

Very rarely does he find insight in thought. It's often when he's not thinking, when he's minding his own business doing nothing, that inspiration strikes.

It happens at the corner shop: inspiration comes free with his garibaldis. Not a petition, he thinks. A pledge. If they get enough signatures from people pledging they'll go to the Screen Seven, maybe the cinema will take note. After all, a petition is just a signature, a pledge is ... well, it may make a difference. Momentarily, in his head, he switches the word *pledge* to *affidavit*, then realising this could be perceived as being stupid, switches it back again.

Much later the whole notion will seem stupid.

It's a light and sunny evening. A cold wind brushes along the street. Outside the corner shop, clutching his biscuits in the wind, he considers extending his trip: continuing his walk and making his way to the supermarket – the shop sells confectionery, papers and biscuits, and not much else; and some food tonight, for dinner, would be more than useful.

He ponders the notion for a while, turning along the street one way towards the supermarket, the other way towards his flat. Then dismisses it, the supermarket being far too busy this time in the evening. He'll make do with what he has.

On his way home, he thinks he's being followed. He turns, intent on asking for a reason, and sees … nobody. He continues on his walk.

Further along the street, thirty metres or so, looking into a travel agent's window, he sees Mark.

He'd thought about this before – a chance meeting with an ex-friend in the street: he'd imagined a time when upon such a meeting he'd engage in conversation, drink coffee, and have a genuinely pleasant time. Now, when it looks like that meeting might actually happen, he finds himself distracted by something in a shop window … lampshades.

Two minutes later it strikes him, first, that he's not interested in lampshades, and then that Mark, too, may be feeling the same way – that he may be looking into the budget travel agent's window in an attempt to avoid contact. In which case they could be staring into windows for a very long time.

A quick glance: Mark has gone.

He feels relief, then a sense of disappointment in himself. Then he feels a series of short stabbing pains in his ribs. A drunken woman has joined him, lampshade-watching, and for reasons not obviously apparent, is prodding him with a biro.

'You're that man,' she tells him, spilling high-strength beer over his shoes, 'on TV,' then continues to prod.

'No I'm not.'

She lodges her beer can in her coat pocket and with her now free, non-pen-jabbing hand, retrieves a stained travelcard from another pocket, which she thrusts at him.

'Sign it.'

'I'm sure you've made a mistake.'

'Awe, go on. You stuck up ponce.'

The rain of light blows to the ribs, now, is making them ache. Withstanding torture not being one of his key skills, not something he'd put on his curriculum vitae, he caves in and agrees to sign. Only, he's not sure who he's supposed to be.

'Now—' he takes the pen and travelcard – 'who am I?'

She laughs.

'You're ...'

Stepping towards him, she takes a closer look.

'No you're not,' she says, and staggers off.

The Lust

Adam flicks through his lists – notes he had made before his big epiphany. He sits reading them while eating a banana.

The top row of every sheet is marked with a name: Steve, Jay, Karen, and so on; twelve friends in total, twelve sheets. It's a small subsection of his acquaintances, but the lists are reserved for the main contenders: the important people, the people who'd consumed most of his time. There are others, of course, who are not on the list, friends and associates to whom Adam had said goodbye to at his farewell party; people that later he may wish he'd kept in contact with. But it's sometimes just easier to start a new life than to fix an old one.

Underneath the name, on each piece of paper, he had written a subheading: 'The List'. For the sheet marked Karen he'd written 'The Lust', black markered it out and written 'The List' underneath in row three (he's not a great believer of the Freudian significance).

Numbers have been scribbled faintly in pencil at the very top of each sheet: one in the left corner, another in the right, and one, a larger figure, in the centre. The figures represent positive attributes, negative attributes, and the balance, the difference between the two.

Adam slides out a drawer built into his kitchen table and takes out a new sheet of paper. At the top of the sheet he writes the word 'Yvette', then starts to copy notes from his work notepad.

He's still filling in her report card when the phone rings. He picks it up. It's Yvette. He can't remember whether he'd given her his home phone number or not. He gives her the benefit.

'We're going canvassing on Thursday,' she tells him.

So she likes this plan of his now does she?

'You hate the plan.'

She admits she'd thought the plan, the canvassing plan, stupid when he'd pitched it, but after some thought she'd realised it not to be as awful as she'd first thought. Besides, here, a stupid plan is better than no plan at all.

'I have to work,' he says, forgetting about the notion of the pledge.

'You have time off to go to the cinema don't you?' There's something about the way she says this which grates.

He flips his notepad back a couple of pages, to a page marked 'Latte Woman', and adds 'demanding' to her list. (He's aware that on occasion this may be a positive but just adds it to her negatives.)

'Yes ... but—'

She interrupts, another attribute, grating in a different way: 'There'll be no point will there, in taking a holiday to watch films if they cancel the programme ... Unless you want to see them in London.'

The thought makes him queasy. She's certainly bossy. That's definitely a negative.

She's right though. He remembers he's already booked a half-day off sick on Thursday, taken the afternoon off for a dentist appointment (normally he would have faked a meeting with a supplier but there had been too many recently and no supplies to show for it). He had planned to go to the cinema – with her, as it happened. He checks his new diary: they had arranged a date.

'Are you changing our date? Or have you forgotten you've made one?'

'Our date?'

'At the cinema, *Amores Perros* at three thirty, Screen Seven?'

She leaves the whole 'no I don't do dates' discussion for another time – though projects disapproval silently, in the gaps between her words. She keeps to the facts.

'It's been cancelled.'

'You cancelled our date without telling me?'

'No, the cinema cancelled the screening.'

This is getting serious. He'd been looking forward to it for weeks. There was little chance of anybody else wanting to see that film at that time (apart from her, and he's fine now with that), and now, for no reason, they've cancelled it. Oh, there's the 'it being not profitable reason', yes; but cancelling a screening at such short notice is most unprofessional.

He wonders if this is a new facet, a new personality trait of hers: dismissing good ideas, then changing her mind. He also wonders if he should mention his new improved plan of asking for pledges rather than signatures.

'Well?' she says.

Canvassing would certainly use up some of his excess time, and in a worthwhile pursuit; and it wouldn't be cyclical, unlike birthdays – he'll not have to do this every year – so his time would not be drained forever. And it would give him time to formulate the plan, about what he really wants to do with this free space in his life. Something relaxing, a hobby, music maybe?

'Well?' she says again, as if she's been kept waiting for minutes – which to be fair, she has.

'Well,' he says, 'as it's my plan, of course I'm in.'

She tells him that although they've started to cancel screenings (and sooner than expected), there's still hope. There is still one more screening to come. *Monsoon Wedding*, an Indian film, will be shown later next week. If they can canvass enough signatures and get enough people to see it, the cinema might reconsider its actions. She uses a lot of aggression when she says this, and is more serious than normal. She says it as if she's giving a pep talk. It doesn't cross her mind that Adam doesn't need to be pepped, or that he might want to do some pepping himself.

And that's it. They arrange to meet on Thursday at 3:30. Not a date, something else completely.

6

Canvassing

They start with the road leading to the cinema. They carry clipboards, forms for signature, lists of the films that have been cancelled, information on the one film that's still going to be screened, and spare pens.

The first pitch goes well. Yvette has a way of getting the importance of the situation across to Mr and Mrs Rice – a pleasant couple in their mid-forties who live at number one. She talks with a passion that makes them actually believe the world will end in chaos, society will crumble, and their two young children will end up in prison by their mid-twenties if they miss out on the film on Thursday. She even offers to find them a babysitter.

'So. Can we count on your support?' she says.

'Yes,' says Mrs Rice, grabbing clipboard and pen from her hand.

She starts to sign, then stops. 'Oh, it hasn't got subtitles in it, has it?'

And here is her first mistake: honesty. There is something else far bigger at stake: humanity, according to her speech. 'Hasn't that got to be worth a small lie?' Adam asks as they leave without the signature.

No, apparently. Yvette wants to persevere with the truth.

The next few houses, most inconsiderately for Adam's liking, the occupants are out. Yvette suspects the homeowners are at work (given they're canvassing in the middle of a workday). They continue along the street.

Next:

A couple in their early twenties watch Yvette's performance. She cuts out three minutes from her last pitch but is heavier with the gesticulation. They are as impressed as Mr and Mrs Rice were earlier, even though they currently have no children to face the prison sentence in years to come.

'Oh, it hasn't got subtitles in it has it?' the woman finally says.

But this time Yvette is more persistent. 'Yes, it has subtitles, like that film *Crouching Tiger, Hidden Dragon* had subtitles. Do you remember?'

Adam's very impressed with this: linking their film to one that's had more success in Screen Seven – he suspects this is the type of film that encouraged the cinema to develop the programme in the first place. There had been one or two 'art film' screenings as they call them, each month, shown on Screen Seven, prior to *Crouching Tiger*, but this film had led to the programme running seven days a week.

'Does it have lots of martial arts in it?' says the man.

'Lots of Kung Fu, and special effects.' The girlfriend raises her arm and jumps into a Kung Fu pose.

'Yes, that's right, it's like *Crouching Tiger*,' Adam says, a comment that Yvette immediately retracts for him, persisting with her honesty plan.

But it works – the *Crouching Tiger* analogy – the couple choosing not to listen to her retraction and signing on the dotted line, taking their petition tally to four.

Four signatures in total: Adam had been the first to sign, quickly followed by Yvette, who had then announced she was going to get her staff to sign, bumping the numbers up further. On the doorstep of their latest signees, Adam, while retrieving his clipboard and pen, wonders who he could get to sign. He doesn't like the idea of sharing a cinema with anybody at all, let alone The Boss or his other colleagues, people that he knew for a fact would bother him. He'd rather take the chance with complete strangers like – he looks at the pledge list – Mark and Doris Knight.

Next:

A bleary-eyed young man opens the door of number twenty-five.

'What?' says the man.

Yvette launches into her speech and is stopped immediately.

'What's the film called?'

Yvette gives him the title and he starts to rant.

'It's elitist claptrap,' says the man, 'designed to oppress the working classes, make them feel inferior because they don't understand it. A waste-of-money-load-of-crappy-toss nobody wants to see unless they're trying to bed some posh bit or pretending to be trendy.'

'It's like *Crouching Tiger Hidden Dragon*,' says Yvette. 'Lots of kicking and fighting.'

'Ohh,' says the man. 'OK, then put me down for two.'

Yvette explains that they're not selling tickets, just

collecting pledges, and they get another signature. The man, a Mr Geoff Porter according to the Print Name box (his signature is illegible), takes the clipboard away, and comes back with three more signatures: Lucy Porter, Jane Porter, and Geoff Porter (senior).

Finding the concept of encouraging others to visit Screen Seven as repugnant as he does, Adam is surprised to find that he's enjoying this canvassing experience. And the people they've talked to so far appear to be the kind of cinemagoers who no doubt would prefer to sit at the back of the cinema rather than at the front with him.

Could he delicately inquire about their usual seating positions and snack-eating habits prior to Yvette's pitch?

He's growing more positive about their chances. Currently he can count four positives: it's an evening performance; it's on a Thursday night; it has had good London reviews; and Yvette's delivery is astounding. As long as these people like opening their doors and watching love, passion, hate, rage and tragedy performed on their doorstep like a great ballet or Shakespearean play, they're assured a victory.

Adam himself takes some of the credit – while Yvette performs her epic, he holds up the poster of the film and points at it while attempting to smile.

They must guard against complacency though. They have only eight signatures so far. And there are the negatives to consider: the one remaining non-mainstream film to be shown at Screen Seven is not an English or American film, and it is subtitled.

Taking a break in the park, they sit on a bench, side by side, sipping take-away teas.

A couple walk past, stop, and mutter to themselves,

glancing occasionally over their shoulders to look at them. An argument develops, the man getting especially animated. Another woman walks past with a child in a push-buggy. Stopped by the couple, she too turns to look at them.

'You see *Amélie?*' asks Adam, seeing the signs, attempting to create a diversion.

'Why are they looking at us?' asks Yvette. 'And what's with the chicken impressions?' In unison the women give him the look: poking heads forward, tensing cheeks and eyes, holding … and relaxing: a kind of he's-not-as-attrac-tive-as-Clive-Owen look only with more aggression. Then they separate: the buggy woman marching off aggressively shaking her head; the couple walking back past them on the bench.

'Never mind, love,' says the woman as she passes, 'you've still got your health ain't ya.'

Yvette, curious, gets up and walks over to the spot on which the women had been impersonating chickens, and looks at Adam.

'No, I can't see it,' she says. 'There's no reason to stand here and impersonate a chicken.'

Next:

A blue door. Adam knocks. A man opens it. Mid-thir-ties and unshaven, he wears an orange bathrobe. Behind the man, a poster of the film *Buffalo '66* hanging proudly on the wall infuses Adam with hope.

Yvette plunges into her speech unaware of the poster, her view obstructed by the man, and the bathrobe – which is too short and showing rather too much upper leg for Adam's liking. She is unaware of the legs too, he notes: if she had been, he would have felt more than a twinge of jealousy.

The man seems genuinely interested in the cinema's change in programming, telling them he normally goes to the cinema in London, where his friends and girlfriend live, but had intended, one day, to try the local facilities.

'What's the film called?' asks the man.

She says, '*Monsoon Wedding.*'

There's a short pause, which she fills, 'Ohh, you'd love it, it's like *Crouching Tiger Hidden Dragon.*'

'No it's not,' the man says. 'I've seen it.'

'Oh,' she says.

'Oh?' Adam says.

'It's about—'

'Please don't tell me what happens,' she interrupts.

Another pause.

'We're not lunatics,' Adam says.

The blue door shuts.

Seduction

The mood is quiet for a while. After the last of her customers leave, Yvette flips over the sign on the door to read 'Closed', and then makes cappuccinos.

'Did you see the film *Amélie*?' Adam asks.

'Yes.'

'What screening?'

'First Thursday, 3:30 performance.'

So there had been somebody there when he saw it.

'Did you see me?'

'Yeah, third row, third seat across.'

'And was there anybody else there, in between us? In the middle?'

'No.' She doesn't need to think.

'Ah.'

They talk to each other about the film, including the bits they didn't like, and agree it would have been better seeing it if there hadn't been so much hype and advertising, which brings him back to the point of his original question. Will they save the French programme? And if so, does that include French-speaking Canadian? (He'd just thought of that – another worry, the load is mounting.) She tells him again that there had only been the two of them in the screening but there would, she imagines, have been a much larger attendance for the evening screening.

'Still, I don't think they'll spare the French,' she says.

'Yes,' he says. 'We should assume not.'

A man raps on the door of the patisserie. Yvette points

to the *closed* sign, and he wanders off.

A long pause, facilitating the slurping of coffee and the vocal sounds of pleasure (Adam's Mmming and Yvette's Ahhhing).

'You're like that actor.'

'Mmmm. Oh yes?'

'Ahh. Yes, the one in that film *The Green Man.*'

'Mmmm. George Cole?'

'Ahh. No no no.'

'Alastair Sim?' He beats her to the name and immediately senses it has aggrieved her: she likes to do the prompting.

'Yes.'

'Ah.'

'Yes ... Not your looks, your voice.'

'Oh.' He knows who Alastair Sim is, but can't recall the voice.

'Of course, you're younger, and more attractive.'

'Oh?'

'Younger, and more attractive than when he was alive ... Alive in his later films, like, err ...' Is this a fluster? The first time he's seen her flustered? He thinks about touching her arm and saying he knows what she means. But she finds her words too quickly: '... err. *The Green Man.*'

'Thank you,' he says, accepting the compliment without dismissing it, without providing a self-deprecating comeback. Until he watches the film, he's not sure how much, exactly, of a compliment it is.

He shows her up to the second floor.

'This light used to flicker on and off,' he says, pointing to the fitting on the communal stairs, then immediately wonders why.

It takes thirty-five seconds to walk up two flights of stairs and in that short time they say nothing. Adam's concern over the sanity of the woman he's about to let into his flat has been gazumped by the greater fear that he'll spend the evening talking rubbish; which makes him remember Michael Cummings paid nine pounds for a notepad. So by the time he opens his door he's starting to feel angry. A mood that stays with him for some time – until Yvette finally says something:

'You know, Peter Lorre's real name was Laszlo Lowenstein.' (She's holding the photograph from *Casablanca*.)

No, he didn't know that.

'You think that's where they got the name Victor Laszlo from?' She sounds excited, as if she's uncovered something (Victor Laszlo is one of the lead characters from *Casablanca*, the film Peter Lorre was working on when the picture had been taken.)

'I don't know.'

'Oh, well, it's probably a common name isn't it?'

'I guess.'

Adam's well aware that a strained conversation may lead to an awkward evening. Their relationship has contained many awkward silences and that's fine – he finds it comforting that neither of them have had to fill them – but awkward conversation is harder to deal with.

'That would have made some film—' she nods at Audrey Hepburn '– those two.'

'Yes it would.'

Yvette, standing by the mantelpiece, studies the photographs for an unfeasible length of time, transfixed by Peter Lorre.

'You can take him out of his frame if you like,' Adam

says as she swings around to face him, 'I have some sheets of A4 paper.'

But she doesn't take him up on his offer. Or ask why she would need the sheets of paper. Rather, she joins him on his two-seater, sitting next to him with no seat in between.

They watch the green fabric in silence. Her eyes flit from mantelpiece to fabric with irregular frequency. As if both items are of such high-intensity interest she's torn between them.

What must she be thinking? A little strange him not watching television but liking film so much? She doesn't comment on the fabric (most people do, his ex-friends certainly). An explanation, it appears, is not required.

He provides one anyway:

'Television – it's a most inferior medium.'

She looks at the fabric.

'It has its upside, yes, for me: I like sitcoms, and *Late Night Poker*, but it's not quite film. OK, I can be sure I'm watching it on my own. And I can sit wherever I like—' the sofa has wheels, and now that his lounge is virtually empty he is able to push it around to any viewing position with ease '– but it's not the same.'

She plays with her hair.

She looks at the photograph.

She looks at the green fabric.

Very strange behaviour, he thinks. Most unlike her. The silence, though, is interesting. Every day, it appears, he observes a completely new kind of silence. How many styles of silence, he wonders, can there be?

'We could … go to the café,' she says, aware of the mood, wanting to move to more familiar surroundings.

'Do you want to?' he says.

'No.'
The silence from earlier repeats itself.

7

Sex and Breakfast

There's something about waking up with somebody he likes which brings out the host in him. After loud morning sex he thinks about breakfast, feels he needs to make an effort. He knows he's still out of supplies but looks in the cupboards anyway: green tea, Ryvita, corned beef – same as yesterday. There are bananas, yes. But he won't offer her one knowing, as he does, the limited appeal of that particular fruit to her – it's not one of her favourites.

He walks to the bakery and picks up fresh croissants, jam, baker's-brand chocolate biscuits and two take-away coffees – much more to his liking.

On the way back, he stops at a video shop: it's closed. The British Comedy section is at the back. He looks towards it, hand cupped against window, baker's tray wedged between body and glass.

Although immediately apparent that without binoculars or some kind of image-enhancing equipment it is impossible to read the covers of the video boxes from such a great distance, he spends a whole five minutes trying – to see a film starring Alastair Sim, that is – but can't.

The tray slips a few inches; he raises his knee for extra support; presses the tray more firmly into the glass. Then, fearing the coffees may be getting cold, he heads back home.

As he returns, he sings as he walks, a high-pitched love song: 'You made my heart sing … with a smile, from afar … love you … love, love, love.' While he's hitting the word 'love' in the song, one of its many occurrences, he bumps into Sockball, his neighbour, in the corridor. He pauses, gives Sockball a nod of recognition, then continues singing (he doesn't want him to think he's stopped singing just because he's been caught): 'Love, love, love, la la la, see, la, la.' Not being able to recall the rest of the words, and conscious he's overdoing it, he stops singing and makes conversation with Sockball.

He's called Sockball after his favourite game. It's the cause of the thudding noise in Adam's flat: Sockball playing that game. He'd played it brazenly in front of Adam the first time they had met, and had asked him to join in: first you have to take off your socks, then roll them into a ball, then throw them at a wall. A pitch, Sockball had called it, like in baseball: elbow up, pull your arm back and throw through the line.

THUD.

They exchange pleasantries, and Adam walks off to his flat singing 'I'm Not In Love' – humming after the first sentence. (He knows he's not in love. The very idea of it. A preposterous notion.)

He returns to find her gone and his corned beef stolen. Wait: wrong cupboard – left cupboard carbohydrates, right cupboard tinned meat products (another of his post-it note sayings) – he finds it in the left; must have moved it hunting for breakfast. He checks the flat again for Yvette, the bathroom and the bedroom – she's still gone. The hallway, the landing, the stairs – nothing.

Sockball's door is half-open. He peeks in, glimpsing sock hitting wall—

THUD.

—but no Yvette.

A minute later his doorbell rings. Answering it, he finds his ex-friend Karen on the doormat. She enters without being invited.

'I don't like thinking that somebody doesn't like me,' she says. 'I don't mind if it's somebody I don't give a damn about but if it's somebody I like?' She sits in an armchair and starts eating croissants from his baker's tray.

'I'm not dumping anybody.'

'Got any sugar for this?' She picks up one of the coffees and removes the lid.

'No,' he says – he'd run out – then finds himself in the kitchen searching for some sachets he'd taken from Yvette's patisserie. He shouts through to the lounge: '… I JUST NEED TO KEEP AWAY FROM EVERYBODY FOR A WHILE …'

In the cutlery drawer he finds the sachets of sugar.

'LOOK,' he shouts, 'I'LL CALL YOU IN SIX MONTHS.' And he means it. In the few days apart from his friends his attitude has mellowed, his tolerance lifted, and he has realised he cares for them, albeit in a not-wanting-to-see-them kind of way.

He returns to the lounge in time to see the television being switched on. Karen has not been hindered by his television-deterrence system. A system that takes him half an hour to dismantle has been taken apart in less than forty seconds. Of course Karen, he observes, has taken a number of short cuts. Yellow post-it notes cover the floor – he doubts whether she's read any of them. The green fabric hangs, part over the arm of the sofa, part in the jam from his baker's tray (jam being the only foodstuff now left in the baker's tray). Paperbacks lie bruised on the carpet. And Charlie the Goldfish and his bowl are now swimming and sitting perilously close to the edge of his bookcase.

He saves Charlie from the same fate as *High Fidelity* and *Nineteen Eighty-Four*, then has a lengthy discussion with Karen on why he would like her to leave, and after watching an episode of *The Good Life* on video (while the television's on), and another coffee, she does.

Being Alastair Sim

His good mood has been somewhat crushed by the morning events. He's thinking of calling in sick, or with an epiphany, when he notices the message on his answer machine: 'Hi. It's me. Just a call to say, yeah, hi. Oh, and sorry I missed breakfast. Had to open up. Didn't think you'd be so long, and umm, pop in, for lunch, if you like. At lunchtime. Yeah, bye.'

Concluding – after assessing the alternatives – that the message is from Yvette (his lover, the woman he'd spent the night with), his good mood resurfaces. It's a mood that will last the whole day and have a disturbing side effect:

In the lobby of his office building, standing next to a distant colleague, he almost feels a compulsion to say hello.

In the lift he actually feels the compulsion. He suppresses it, and is relieved when the man gets out on the first floor. One more and he'd be in friend-making territory.

He spends the rest of the day staying away from the Danger Zones. He'll not be queuing next to anybody for a while.

On his way home he buys some bananas, food for Charlie, and a video. He considers a trip to the supermarket and dismisses the idea – the television's still set up after Karen's little visit and he wants to make use of it.

He watches the video: *The Green Man*, with Alastair Sim. Starring Alastair Sim, that is. Adam likes being compared to him, he'll rent more of his movies – that one where he's with a bunch of crooks, lodging together for seven days?

No, he can't remember the name. She would know.

After resetting the television-avoidance system, he puts a small mirror on the kitchen table, wedges it between two large books so it stands erect, sits, and peers into it, copying Alastair Sim mannerisms from the film – eyebrow movements mainly, along with the odd phrase. He likes it. Thinks it fun. He takes another mirror from the bathroom and positions it at a right angle to the first, then moves his head so he can see his face from front and side at the same time. He stands up and leisurely walks a circuit of the table, muttering phrases from the film, sits, looks into the mirror and moves his eyebrows while saying, 'Yes, inspector.' (He can't recall whether Alastair Sim had actually said those words in that film: it isn't one of the phrases he'd just practised. The correct words may have been 'yes, constable', or 'yes, sergeant'; he is sure, though, that Alastair Sim must have said 'yes, inspector' in one of his films.)

He repeats this time after time, walking the kitchen table circuit, muttering, sitting, then saying, 'Yes, inspector.'

Pace. Mutter. Sit. Eyebrows: 'Yes, inspector?'

He says it questioningly, sarcastically, with bemusement, in a how-dare-you-disturb-me tone. Still, it's not right. He can't find the right look.

After a number of minutes, the quality of his Alastair Sim has not improved. It should be an easy affair; he's constantly told he looks like people, and Yvette believes he has the mannerisms of this fellow. Yet, after sitting and looking into the mirror and muttering, he feels no impact. He just looks like himself pulling a stupid face.

He perseveres, varying the delivery again, saying it inquisitively, cynically, and in a variety of tones intended to imply he does not want to be disturbed.

'Yes, inspector' (baffled).

'Yes, inspector' (with bravado).

'Yes, inspector' (with a wink).

'Yes, inspector' (with his hands cupped over his ears).

No, he can't find the look. There must be something else. It's not just about eyebrows and forehead. There's more to being Alastair Sim than you'd think.

In the lounge he assesses the situation. Looking at green fabric, then his watch, he deliberates whether there's enough time to re-watch the video. There isn't.

The police had stopped him once (another case of mistaken identity) but he can't remember what he'd said to them – probably just 'What?' Or 'Yes?' It's unlikely he would have made reference to the policeman's rank. He can only hope to be stopped again one day, so he can try out this new phrase of his.

The circuit evolves throughout the evening, elongating, expanding; the route takes him through the kitchen door, along the corridor, through one lap of the lounge and back to the kitchen, where, he observes, there has been a change to his fridge magnets.

Definitely, yesterday they had read 'she fancies you'. Now they read 'I fancy you'. (This he checks by cross-referencing with his television post-it notes.)

Between bouts of being Alastair Sim, he spends several cups of tea deliberating who has been rearranging his things. He's had two visitors recently, an ex-friend and a lover. One of them has changed his magnets.

Is Yvette the kind of woman who'd rearrange his personal possessions without asking him? Probably. She could have wandered into his kitchen this morning, looking for him, and decided to change his magnetic letters.

He'd left her in bed, Yvette. He remembers clearly asking if she wanted coffee. Then he remembers getting up and getting her coffee (and breakfast – from the bakery). Then he remembers his ex-friend Karen appearing and drinking Yvette's coffee.

Did, at any point, Karen enter the kitchen? He can't recall. They had watched that television programme, *The Good Life* – what did she do in that commercial break?

And 'fancy' is a word that Karen is very fond of. It's a word he heard so often when they first met that Adam now finds it's part of his own vocabulary. He too now uses the word, quite against his will, and far too often. The word's just a bit too young for him, isn't it? At the age of thirty he thinks he needs a new one.

Pace. Mutter. Sit. Eyebrows: 'Yes, inspector?'

8

Orange Snaps

Adam smells biscuits. Somebody, in the last five minutes, has eaten an orange snap (a crunchy biscuit with orange-scented filling).

He looks at Sockball: would it be impolite to ask for one? Or has he pushed his neighbour's goodwill to the limit? Adam had asked if he could watch television with him, and he'd agreed. At the time, he thought Sockball was going to watch the sitcom *Frasier*. But Sockball had only sent out that impression to his neighbours.

Adam had definitely heard the opening soundtrack to *Frasier* as he had walked past Sockball's door (as Alastair Sim), and now thinks that it was during the time between the knocking and the answering that the channel had been changed.

As he can see no orange snap biscuits in the vicinity, and thinking now that he could be wrong in his assumption that the biscuits had been here at all (he sees a bowl of what looks like orange potpourri by the television), he refrains from asking. His life this evening is full of disappointment.

'So. You don't watch *Frasier* then?'

'No.'

The visit from his ex-friend Karen and the subsequent watching of television has increased his craving for sitcoms. An uncontrollable impulse has put him in a precarious situation: it's hard enough to avoid friendships when talking about television, and here he is now watching it with a fellow.

Apparently his host doesn't watch much television (a thing they have in common). Sockball only watches the news, and cookery programmes located outdoors, and factual documentaries incorporating woodland scenery. These viewing habits he regulates through will-power alone – a quality Adam finds admirable: it's another dangerous sign.

Sockball also provides a conducive environment in which to be Alastair Sim. Adam had been caught this morning in the corridor while practising his impersonation, and Sockball hadn't said anything – except 'Hello'. Oh, to Sockball, Adam may have just looked like a man walking the corridor – there's the chance he appeared merely his normal self; but at the end of his circuit, after sitting, muttering, and saying 'Yes, inspector' into his mirrors, Adam had definitely felt a twinge of Alastair Sim. So it must have been a good impression – he's made a lot of progress, very quickly, and it's only a question of time before his impression is recognised.

You see how easy it is? Common ground is found too easily. It's easy to spot the positives in a fellow when you don't know him, isn't it? Especially when you think he's about to watch *Frasier*, and you're acting on autopilot, and you've got an uncontrollable compulsion to watch sitcoms, and you've got a time-consuming television-prevention system (time-consuming, that is, when you don't take short-cuts which may endanger your aquatic pets).

What was he thinking?

They watch a cookery entertainment programme to-gether, which is a negative – the only one, but a big one: it's the only form of televisual entertainment Adam's averse to. Other programmes he can dislike yet watch in a trance-like state all day; cookery entertainment makes him queasy.

It's a relief when after just one episode (he notes during the commercial break that the digital channel is showing several episodes back-to-back) the set is switched off. Adam makes his excuses and leaves.

Back home he deliberates: could he be trying to sabotage his new-found freedom? One moment of weakness and he could be lumbered, befriended. He'll be more vigilant from now on. It's so easy to recreate a problem once you've es-caped from it; and it's easier to avoid a friendship than to relieve oneself of their company.

Sitting back in his comfy sofa, he watches the green fab-ric. His impulse to watch sitcoms has passed.

It's not the only dangerous situation he has found him-self in recently. The other day, in the lift, Adam almost said hello to somebody. It's not the kind of attitude he normally has. Obviously, he wasn't thinking about the conse-quences. It was an impulse that felt quite natural at the time even though it's quite out of character. Adam can only pre-sume he'd been softened by events, by Yvette, and resolves to make more of a conscious effort to keep to his princi-pals.

He's not one of those habitual friend-seekers. He doesn't need new friends just because he's stopped seeing the old ones. Besides, he's taking a friendship holiday: six months without them.

Really, he's escaped lightly: a couple of conversations about clothes colour and dyeing techniques with Steven; a good-luck-on-your-trip card from Mark; a phone call each from Jay and Karen, and that's it – difficult, but over with. No more friends. And the longer he is in his new life the more he likes it. A clean start.

There will be stressful moments to come, no doubt. He's bound to bump, again, into Mark in the street; forced into a conversation about Australia. He'll be unable to avoid it. He'll not try to avoid it. If fate demands another meeting, he'll go along with it. They'll have tea together – Mark's a nice enough fellow. But that is it: a line in the sand: a cup of tea given a chance meeting.

The others too: Steven and Jay and Karen and the rest. Tea and chat with ex-friends. He'll have to set boundaries, of course, there'll be no talk of weddings or anniversaries, none of those old conversation topics that drove him crazy. A strict ten-minute time limit. No invitations to events, no put-downs, or disparaging remarks about his attire. He could take them to the café!

Of course, they don't frequent establishments serving non-alcoholic beverages. So he doubts they'd take him up on his kind offer; but if they do happen to meet, his new attitude may do something to reduce the guilt he feels at the clumsy way he told them he no longer wished to see them.

He did, though, keep a little dignity, telling the truth in his goodbye speech. It would have been harder if he had lied. If he'd told people he was, say, going to travel. Or that he was going to prison – yes that would have been a good one; but he hadn't thought of it, and is averse to—

Adam is disturbed by a knock at the door.

Abduction – Another Case
of Mistaken Identity

He keeps calm and listens for voices, something he'll be able to identify them by later. But they drive off in silence.

The car itself? A white Mercedes, he thinks but can't be sure: he'd only had a glimpse in the hallway before they strapped a blindfold on. What make of Mercedes he can't say; he's not interested in cars but it's certainly a common type – two of his ex-friends have them. He thinks of consulting them later about the matter, then dismisses the notion: he's had one week with minimal contact; talking to them now, about cars, would complicate things. Besides, he's not been hurt as such, and is finding the whole experience somewhat exciting.

The boot of the car smells, an earthy smell: grass? dirt? clay? A mixture of all three? Hardly useful so far.

He'll ask for the inspector when he escapes; it'll give him a chance to practise his line. He tries his Alastair Sim:

'Yes, inspector?' Somehow, it doesn't sound the same with his mouth gagged.

But what to tell the police? That he's been bundled into the boot of what may have been a white Mercedes by some figures in black, and that the boot has an earthy smell and … he feels something jarring against his back … and contains a pick-axe! No. He couldn't expect them to make an arrest on that.

And he can hardly expect the figures to make it easy for him: it's not customary for kidnappers to wear nametags.

What else? They're not very good at tying gags – he works it loose easily and primes himself to call for help at the right moment. He listens intensely: nothing.

Adam's hardly bothered by this matter. He doesn't even find it inconvenient, assuming as he does, another case of mistaken identity. He continues to listen for clues as to where he's being taken, noises that may provide a link to the abductors' hideout. And he hears ... the noise of traffic.

After twenty minutes of traffic noise, he hears the noise of no traffic, the noise of the car stopping, of footsteps, and of the car boot opening.

It's dusk when his blindfold is removed – he's in a red clay quarry, on his knees, hands bound behind his back, the gag loosely hanging round his neck. A semi-circle of figures surround him, all dressed in black, except one, whose balaclava has a distinctly purple tint. There's a mound of earth to his left, and a man-sized hole in the ground ahead.

Purple Tint, presumably their leader, steps forward, pulls a notepad from his pocket, and starts reading:

'You have been excommunicated from our friendship.'

'Steven?'

Steven stops speaking and looks directly at Adam. A voice from the semi-circle, Jay's voice, eggs him on.

The abductors form into a group huddle, as if on some team-building exercise, and start to mumble.

'Steven, what are you doing?'

The group carry on mumbling.

Adam knows Steven likes to think of himself as a Robert De Niro character, a bit of a hard man in pursuit of respect.

More mumbling.

But he's not usually somebody who'd organise any sort of activity that doesn't involve large amounts of alcohol.

'You're not the mafia,' Adam says, trying to elicit some attention. 'You're not the mafia. You're just a group that goes to the pub. A lot.'

'Don't get personal,' says Steven, in the high-pitched voice he takes on when he's stressed.

Steven's favourite film is *Casino*, he loves the gruesome ending: gangsters beat somebody up with baseball bats, throw him in a shallow grave, and bury him alive.

'Sinatra, Dean Martin, the Rat Pack, that's what gangsters listen to,' Adam shouts, trying without success to get to his feet. 'They don't listen to *The Monkees*.'

Adam, attempting to get up, falls flat onto the red clay earth, closer to the hole in the ground.

They ignore him. The huddle breaks and Steven, full of energy after his pep talk, takes his place at the centre of the semi-circle.

'I can't see Robert De Niro singing "Daydream Believer",' Adam shouts, his face scrubbing against red clay, 'it's not quite his style.'

Steven reads mechanically from his notepad: 'You, Adam King, have been excommunicated from our friendship. We shall not see you or speak to you again. With the exception of birthdays, weddings and anniversaries.' The notebook is snapped shut.

'Look. People. You do not need me. I'm just friend filler, I just make up the—'

'It took me two hours to dig that hole,' Jay interrupts, his voice saturated with irritability.

Jay and a few others in the clan have become increasingly restless since their group huddle: fidgeting, stepping out of alignment, twitching, and generally ruining what looks to be a good semi-circle formation. A formation which no doubt they have practised; the synchronised aggression had initially – once the blindfold had been removed – made Adam feel uneasy.

'Sorry—' Adam peeks into the hole – 'it's a very good hole. Really well dug.'

'Clay's not as easy to dig as you'd think.'

'I'm touched, you've obviously gone to a lot of trouble.' Adam looks along the line of figures. 'But I'm not going to rejoin your group. So you're going to have to kill me.'

Adam is quite right: they had gone to a great deal of effort in setting up this little charade. It had been a long day of digging holes, filling holes in, and visiting garden centres. Many of them are tired and irritable. This is not the first hole they had dug (Jay had dug). The first had been in a park near Adam's house; they had been moved on by the police and had been lucky to escape with a caution; their spade also had been confiscated. (Jay's spade.) They had moved to a second park – where another spade had been confiscated, (their second spade), by a keeper who'd been on his way to call the police when they'd made a run for it.

There had also been expenses: petrol, masks, tying-up equipment are much more expensive than you'd think, and although they'd arranged a kitty, the management of the expense budget was forming seeds of discontent. Jay wondered if he'd ever recover the cost of his original spade, an expense the group (Steven) had overlooked.

Adam, too, now starts to feel tired.

'OK. What do you want me to say? That I don't like you? That we have nothing in common? That I wish you'd just go away.' This isn't true, but tiredness has an effect: it makes him grumpy.

He retracts the statement immediately – something that'll annoy him later – and tries to persuade people that they've got him wrong, that he's a bad friend, a bad listener, self-obsessed, somebody you wouldn't want to know – he just gives out a good impression. He's just lucky. Hearing the words leave his mouth, he knows they sound patronising but can't stop himself. He almost enjoys it. He gets carried away, annoyed that he'd retracted that statement a moment ago, a statement which applies to some of the group at least. He retracts his retraction.

'OK. I don't like you. We have nothing in common. I do wish you'd go away.'

And they do – after more mumbling, huddling, and discussion, they turn their backs and peel, in clusters, from the semi-circle.

Making way to their cars, two figures comfort each other in a warm display of affection he's never seen from them before: a very public hug. One of the pair breaks contact and takes a few heavy steps back towards Adam.

'You told me you were going to Australia.'

Adam feels like saying sorry, but resists: 'No, Mark, I didn't.'

And that's it. He's left in the quarry, alone. It takes him an hour to untie himself and three more to get home.

9

Peter and Audrey

He'd arrived home at 5:30. Three hours' sleep, and for some reason, on waking, he's quite keen on work. Going to work.

Aware that sleep deprivation may invoke delirium – after a hectic night it would be more appropriate to call in sick – he curbs his excitement and sleeps for another half-hour.

On waking, still a desire to go to the office. It is most unusual for him. But he's focused, there is much to do: petition forms to create, flyers to print, schedules to organise. A campaign to run.

First he spends some time thinking, pacing, and being Alastair Sim. Venturing into the hallway he extends his circuit: past the door of Sockball, to the end of the corridor this time before returning, passing his own door, passing the door of High-Pitched Squeak Man, to the top of the stairs, and back to his flat.

Then he goes to work.

Queuing for the photocopier – he always does his own

photocopying, especially when he's copying flyers asking people to save the Screen Seven programme – he is aware of the risk he is taking: queuing in a danger area, a place where conversations start far too easily. These areas should come with warnings he thinks, queuing for five minutes without being bothered.

More people join the queue, men from marketing, women from accounts and administration. Conversations to the left of him, conversations to the right, but within five minutes, clutching his flyers, he emerges unscathed.

It's a strenuous day; avoiding the company of the television-talkers and the friend-makers proves tiresome, but the trip to the quarry last night has strengthened his resolve – his new life beckons.

After a short communication with his boss in which he succeeds in not absorbing any information at all except a swear-word count of thirteen (which includes two brand-new ones), he heads back home, taking his photocopying with him. On the way he stops beside each tree, bends slowly at the knees, deposits the flyers on the pavement, takes the top copy, and staples it to the bark. The twenty-six trees on his journey have little impact on his pile of flyers.

At home, briefly he feels a little self-conscious at not having any friends to invite on his street-calling expeditions.

Pace. Mutter. Sit. Yes, inspector?

The feeling dissolves.

Is it too much, he wonders, to want a life in which he is surrounded by people who know they're not in the mafia? Who have no inclination to be in the mafia? People who are just content being themselves.

Pace. Mutter. Sit. Yes, inspector (baffled).

There should be a test: Do you own a gun? Is your name Al, Rob, Mr Pink? Can you speak mafia? Do you even like Italian food? Have you ever broken the law in any way? Do you work in the meat-packing business? In gambling? Are you wanted for extortion? Murder? Tax evasion?

In those gangster films, the good ones, you're not allowed to leave the family. Once you're in there's no way out. Once you're family, you're always family. It's just like, well, family. You're stuck with them: weddings, anniversaries, Christmas.

His ex-friends, they have many overlapping negative attributes, and positive, but have only four negatives in common: negatives they all possess to varying extents.

ONE: They're too fond of criticising others.

TWO: They're miss-matchers. A particular type of personality who believes it's fun to take the opposite point of view to anybody they're talking to with a belligerent belief they are omnipotent and know the truth about everything. It's a type of sport.

THREE: They find it impossible to comprehend that another human being is unable to tolerate alcohol. (See Quality Two.)

FOUR: They think they're in the mafia.

At his kitchen table, he is scouring his notes, searching for his list of their common positives, when he's disturbed by Yvette.

'Come quick,' she says, marching in and pulling at his shirtsleeve, unbalancing him slightly as he tries to cover his notes.

Shuffling the papers into a pile, he smiles at her while regaining his balance, then discreetly returns them to their hiding place – the secret drawer in the kitchen table.

A moment or two later they're in the lounge, looking at his photographs.

'What?'

'Oh.' She steps to the mantelpiece, takes hold of Audrey Hepburn from one end of the mantelpiece and Peter Lorre from the other, and, while making an appropriate sound effect, she pulls them together.

'Tan-nar!'

Peter and Audrey are now in the centre, squished side by side on the mantelpiece, facing out over the lounge. To-morrow they'll be joined by a vase of flowers and some knick-knacks.

Turning, she sees his reaction.

'Thought you would like it,' she says, taking him by the hand now, leading him towards the bedroom.

And do you know, he does.

Television Aversion Therapy

The next evening, a panic: he finds his compulsion has returned. Green fabric in hand, standing over the television set, he thinks about watching *The Green Man* with Alastair Sim. (It's difficult to be this fellow when you've only seen the film once; interest can wane very quickly without inspiration.) Also tonight, on television, a late-night screening of *The Belles of St Trinian's* (yes, starring him), followed by some other stuff that may be watchable, and *Late Night Poker*.

A slippery slope? He re-covers the television set.

What's brought on this relapse he can't say. His day had been an enjoyable one – a relatively calm day at work, lunch with Yvette, canvassing in the afternoon – nothing to induce this kind of desire. There had been the usual television talk at work – he'd been subjected to it at the photocopier and in the lobby – but nothing more than usual.

A distraction is required.

Pace. Mutter. Sit. 'Yes, inspector?'

Through into the kitchen he paces; without stopping, without looking down, he picks up a glass of water by the sink and continues on his circuit as Alastair Sim, sipping from the glass as if at a cocktail party he doesn't want to be at.

Mutter. Mutter. Sip. Sip. Pace. Sit. 'Yes, inspector?'

Of course, people may not know who Alastair Sim is. A lot of people do not. It's of no concern to him. (Adam himself has only seen a couple of his films.)

Questions may be asked about the person he's impersonating and more importantly, why; he will deal with them if they arise.

After a number of revolutions of his flat – after looking into his mirrors and saying 'Yes, inspector' in a variety of subtexts – he finds himself again standing by the television set, green fabric draped over his arm, looking at the yellow post-it notes that swamp the television screen.

A bigger distraction may be required:

Sockball answers the door in bare feet and invites him in.

Three pairs of socks lie on the table.

'Would you like to play?' Sockball points at them. 'They're clean.'

'No. No, that's OK.'

'Well, do you mind if I?'

'No. Go ahead.'

THUD.

It's unlike Adam to be overly friendly. Yes, you can be friendly to a man without being his friend. Friendly does not convey the notion of friendship. And anyway, Sockball is a neighbour, not a friend. And he's allowed neighbours in this new life he's inventing, isn't he. He can hardly avoid them. Nor should he when the man watches those obscure science and nature and cookery programmes. The kind of programme Adam takes offence at.

Let's call it television-aversion therapy. Last time he sat on Sockball's sofa the programme he was forced to endure made him pleased he was on his television abstinence programme.

Only, Adam isn't watching the kind of programme that gives him indigestion and makes him feel sick and makes him want to not watch television. And he's not watching the kind of programme he can stand (any other programme). He's watching—

THUD.

—He's watching socks hit wall.

THUD.

The vibration causes a pair – one of the spare pairs – to roll slowly off the edge of the table. Adam watches it fall, and is about to pick them up when he thinks better of it.

He spends the rest of the evening not watching television, with his neighbour.

The next morning he meets with Yvette, spending three hours canvassing and collecting ten more signatures.

The weather grows cold and blustery while they talk and walk and pitch prospective cinemagoers, and it rains intermittently – the stormy weather adds to the tragedy of her performance. Her pitch comes in three acts today and receives several standing ovations. Adam's workload also increases: he not only holds the umbrella but has to catch her during her fainting scene.

While they move from house to house – as the storm grows stronger and the umbrella proves inadequate for the conditions – Yvette gets into the habit of holding his hand. A positive, Adam will think later? Or a negative. He will be undecided.

When the storm grows too heavy, they return to Adam's apartment and sit side by side on Adam's sofa, towel-drying their hair and looking at the fabric that hangs over his television set. The room is quiet, except for the sounds of chimpanzees and large apes and flute music. Adam assumes his neighbour Sockball is watching the science and nature channel.

Adam dunks a bourbon cream, or more precisely dips it (dunking this kind of biscuit has a tendency to create wastage, unless you're the type who enjoys fishing soggy biscuit from your tea). Holding it in mid-air, he waits for it to dry, and relaxes.

Yvette, sitting next to him (fidgeting constantly), gets up, walks around the sofa, behind Adam, bends down over his shoulder and peers at his biscuit hanging in mid-air, almost dry, ready for consumption. She makes a movement towards him, as if to kiss him, then eats the biscuit.

This partly had been expected: the same thing had happened to his last biscuit, just two minutes ago.

Their meetings will become increasingly passionate, and cutesy – a behaviour that Adam will take time adjusting to, but will eventually like it, miss it when it's not there.

Over the following week she'll invent a cute name for him and expect one in return. When she's not given one, she'll invent one herself and pretend he gave it to her.

They spend the rest of the evening not watching television, and talking about saving Screen Seven.

Frankenstein

Sitting at his kitchen table, he looks at his breakfast: grilled corned beef in Ryvita crispbread, a cup of green tea and a banana – same as yesterday. He'll not be eating the banana until he gets to work, but keeps it with his breakfast on the table – it adds to the aesthetics: the square brown table, the white plate, the brown crispbread, the brownish melted corned beef, the green cup, the yellow banana. Oh, and the envelope (a letter which, he notes, does not have a postmark). The items on the table can be rearranged in any position – plate in the centre with cutlery, tea to his right, banana to the left, post over to the side – it doesn't matter, the table retains its aesthetic. What is important is that he eats his crispbread while it's hot, before the corned beef solidifies. (This is of course purely conjecture on his part – he's never eaten a solidified crispbread, but why take the risk?)

He takes a bite, straightens his spine slightly, adding an inch or two to his sitting height, and pauses: the saltiness, the gooiness, the crunch, it gives him a natural high. (It's quite puzzling when you think about it: two products he dislikes individually combining to provide such a thrill.)

Until recently he's always been a bit snobbish about it, the food in his cupboards; his tinned meat products were always stored behind the carbohydrates and only eaten in emergencies, like today. Recently, though (after he'd eaten this concoction for the first time), he'd rearranged his cupboards. It was a simple task given his limited stock: two tins of corned beef and a few slices of crispbread. (His bananas – which he notes are dwindling in number – are kept on a special stand on the work surface, beneath the cupboards.)

Sipping his tea, he looks at his mail – a postcard of Australia. He clamps it to the fridge door with a magnet. The card isn't signed – it's blank, except for a large question mark.

Had he given up people before? Girlfriends possibly? Actually he'd always split by mutual consent – there had been little drama even in those conditions (until now); situations would deteriorate to such an extent that breaking up had always been the logical and natural thing to do. So he's had no experience in these things at all, from either side; he excuses his clumsiness, his lack of communication, his lack of diplomacy, the manner in which he conducts himself with those ex-friends. He won't berate himself. It's a life skill he needs to learn.

Washing his plate, cup and cutlery, looking out of the kitchen window, Adam's concerns over Yvette's sanity resurface. He thinks about their first night together: the night they'd first slept together. After canvassing, and after coffees at the patisserie, they'd decided to reconvene at his flat to discuss stage two of their plan, and she had led the way. Clearly she had known not only the street on which he lives but the apartment block too. Also she had phoned him at home. So she'd known his home phone number.

All relationships have baggage, though – don't they? This again is where friends come in handy. If he wasn't on this friendship sabbatical he could call up a friend and they could tell him the obvious: that the woman's obviously some kind of lunatic, that for once he really is being followed, and that he shouldn't date her. And he could tell the friend that she says she doesn't do dates. And his friend could say, 'But she's dating you isn't she?'

And after putting down the phone, he could remember he had been wrong before – that there had been a perfectly logical reason for her knowing about where he works. That she'd known this because she sees him there sometimes, when she looks through the window of the patisserie, she sees him in his boss's office.

Adam finishes the washing up. After drying his hands, he finds his friends' lists and adds a positive to each of their totals.

They have their positives, his friends: Jay's insistence that Adam looks like some film star is both flattering and endearing. Karen – have you met Karen? Yes, of course; well, Karen has her positives too. You'll see. All his friends have both sides: the negatives and the positives.

OK. They seem OK, don't they – his friends. They seem good people; and they are. They're just a little different to Adam. And they hide them well, their negatives, keep them hidden, submerge them until you're vulnerable. Not on purpose – don't be ridiculous – but they're there.

The good points – there are lots of them. It's just, well, they're outnumbered. And the good and bad parts are stuck together – at a molecular level.

He misses his Frankenstein friend: a friend he makes up sticking together personality parts of his old friends: supportive, kind, uplifting. A genetically modified good friend, that's what he needs. On paper it's easy to create. First you create a new list, then transplant the positive attributes of your old friends onto it. This creates the perfect person: A Frankenstein friend, a positive monster. But what happens to the leftovers, where do you keep the negative traits? You can't just dispose of them; they bind together and form monsters of their own.

Anyway, the Frankenstein friend doesn't exist, and Adam suspects that despite recent advancement in genetics it will be some years before he has an opportunity to create one. So there's a choice: he can take their good side and their bad, or take neither. He can't just throw out personality traits. If he's to have the uplifting, positive side of those friends, he must also deal with their negative sides; if he's to see the good monster, he must also talk to the bad ones. There can be no body parts, no personality traits, left over.

His subconscious provides him with a ratio: three bad Frankenstein Monsters to one good one.

10

Agony Aunt

A particularly noisy bird keeps him awake – chirping out of tune. It must be the only bird in the world that can't hit a note. He checks his watch: two thirty in the morning. Isn't it a bit early for dawn chorus?

Leaving Yvette in bed, he gets up, pulls on socks, pants and T-shirt and peers through the bedroom window. He can just make the thing out, hiding in the tree, as if it knows it's being a nuisance.

It's dark – he sticks his head out of the window, accustoming himself to the light. Dawn, quite clearly, is not about to arrive.

How's the poor creature going to find a mate?

The bird flits to another branch, further away now, but in plain view. More importantly, it shuts up.

It's too early to be calling the opposite sex. The other birds aren't up yet. That's if they're here at all: don't blackbirds migrate? Who knows?

He looks around – it appears to be the only bird awake.

It flits nearer and starts singing at him. A sort of off-key screeching chirp. The kind that sets teeth on edge and makes you want to stick your head under a pillow. A unique noise with no beat. A noise he's never heard from a bird before. A noise that shouldn't exist any more. You'd think they'd have died out millions of years ago, tone-deaf blackbirds. Genetics should have seen to that. What-do-you-call-it, the Darwin factor. Millions of years of selective breeding and this bird's probably the only one left, its genes spared by evolution.

He watches it with envy. Because finding a mate if you're a blackbird requires little analysis. You've either got a good voice, or you haven't. And if you haven't, what's the point? Move on. Do something else with your life. Stop thinking about it.

The bird keeps chirping.

Of course the poor creature doesn't realise he's got no chance.

Now that Adam has a love life of his own, he feels somehow entitled to give advice on the matter and speaks to the bird at length. Then, realising it is highly unlikely the bird will follow any of the dating advice he is offering – chirping lessons, getting up at a more reasonable time, taking its holidays in the south of France with all the other birds – he goes back to bed.

Yvette, half asleep, warm and sweaty, hugs him and, dribbling over his shoulder, makes a half comment about him being a sweet man before falling back to sleep. Adam, though, stays awake for a while, wondering how sound his advice had been. His knowledge in matters of love may be improving but he knows little about science and nature (is that what blackbirds do – go to the south of France?). He needs guidance.

———

'That's a Chilean,' Sockball tells him, excited, looking out of his kitchen window.

'Is it?' Adam says. *A Chilean blackbird, my, my.*

'Not the bird, the tree,' Sockball says, reading Adam's mind. 'It's a Chilean cedar.'

Sockball disappears into another room and returns with a book. 'Look,' he says, pointing at a picture.

'Oh, yes,' Adam says, perturbed that he finds this interesting. 'What about the blackbird?'

'I don't have a book on blackbirds,' Sockball says. 'I don't know anything about them.'

Adam is surprised that Sockball hasn't heard the blackbird with the off-pitch chirp. Surely it's loud enough to keep anybody awake. From the layout of his neighbour's flat, Adam guesses that Sockball's bedroom is a mere twenty feet further to the right of the tree than his own, comfortably within the ear-splitting range of the feathered screecher, and yet when Adam had knocked to discuss the matter, Sockball had been fast asleep. The whole thing Adam finds very suspicious.

They spend the early morning hours looking at the tree.

After a breakfast meeting with Yvette, Adam walks into a meeting with The Boss.

'I'm telling you, I'm not F***ING having it. Those C***S won't rip me off. You understand?'

'I understand,' says Adam, forgetting to zone out and trapping himself in a conversation with his nemesis, preoccupied as he is with other matters. He peeks out of the window to see if he can see her, berates himself for being a sap when he can't, and moves his chair from the window, avoiding further distraction.

'And where were you this morning, you C**T.'

'Oh, I had a breakfast meeting with a supplier.'

'And who paid for that?'

'They did.'

'Good. Well, if there's free food going, you let me know next time. C***S. And next time you eat double everything.' The Boss's posture springs to life: 'If they're spending cash on you, they're sweating. F*** 'em.'

In his experience with this company, the most important thing you can do is turn up at a regular time. To be punctual. But now he appears to have found a way to bypass that law completely: an encouraging start to the day, he thinks, patting his coat pockets, searching for his morning banana.

He spends the rest of the morning sharpening his collection of pencils and arranging them in height order.

Adam leaves work two hours early (earlier than originally planned, that is). He decides to start canvassing without Yvette and is walking towards the cinema when he becomes aware of a disturbance.

Somebody behind is shouting at him, shouting the word 'Harley'. Adam turns to confront the fellow: he's in no mood for signing autographs while there are signatures to collect. He has no time to waste on the insane or the drunk or people wanting him to sign bus passes; there'll be no more going along with their cases of mistaken identity – unless somebody picks up on his Alastair Sim.

Turning around, he sees this man isn't a tramp, or insane, or even talking to him, but Adam turns his ear towards the fellow just in case:

'Harley. Harley Macbeth, you come here now!'

And people have the cheek to think him a lunatic. Adam, conscious of the task ahead, is about to be on his way when the man does speak to him:

'Oi, geeza, you seen Harley?' he says.

Adam's quite sure he's never met anybody of that name and is about to tell him so when he's shushed.

'Shhhh,' says the man, then listens very hard and with a slight stupor. 'You hear it?'

They listen – nothing. Except, Adam detects, number 17 watching *Quincy*. More information is required:

'Hear what?'

'Geeza!' the man says, looking at Adam as if he were an idiot. 'Cat noises: Meows! Purring! Noises made by cats!'

They listen – there are no cat noises.

The man shows Adam a picture of a white cat.

'Have you seen him – Harley, my cat?'

Adam looks at the picture and, after a morning of listening to his boss, wonders how much more useless information his brain will have to accommodate – brain space he needs for other matters.

'You seen *Monsoon Wedding*?'

'What's that? Your cat?' He shows Adam his picture again.

Adam explains about the film; he runs through his routine, and after several rude interruptions regarding the whereabouts of a certain young moggy, says: 'I'll tell you whether I've seen your cat or not if and after you see *Monsoon Wedding*.'

The Cat Man quietly slides his photograph back into his coat pocket.

'And I'll need proof. A ticket stub will suffice.'

Then, sensing that he's hurt the young man's feelings, he caves in, tells him he's not seen his cat. And that he's an animal lover.

'I have a goldfish,' he says, trying to alleviate the Cat

Man's suspicion.

'And if you want I can ask around while I'm canvassing, ask if anybody's seen it ... If you have a spare photograph?'

But he has only one.

They spend the next hour searching together, for Harley. After the hour, conscious of his own task this evening and believing that he's provided enough assistance to cancel out any negative karma which may have arisen earlier, Adam bids the Cat Man good day. At a fork in the road they separate, the Cat Man continuing to look for his pet, Adam knocking on doors and pitching people about saving Screen Seven.

It's an experience Adam had found to be more draining than he had expected, looking for the cat: under cars on hand and knee, through muddy gardens, poking around dustbins, climbing through thorn bushes. All for no gratitude, not even a thank you as they part.

A few doors later, after an unsuccessful pitch to a group of teenage boys (his pitch is improving, but he doesn't have quite the same dramatic punch as Yvette), he turns to see the Cat Man again. Pointing at him. And accompanied by a policeman.

The policeman asks whether he's seen the gentleman's cat.

'No,' Adam says.

And it's not until a few hours later, while he's polishing and rearranging his photographs of Peter Lorre and Audrey Hepburn, that he sees his missed opportunity.

OK, so the policeman wasn't an inspector, he was a constable, but it had been a good opportunity to practise his Alastair Sim in a real life situation, and they are very infrequent.

He puts his behaviour and his missed opportunity down

to stress. Consider this: there are only a few more days to save Screen Seven, and the consequences of failure are too distressing to contemplate. So far they've gained a mere twenty-five signatures.

Help is required.

He asks Sockball.

'No,' Sockball says, 'I'm not a 2-D entertainment type of man. I like my entertainment 3-D, that's why I like sockball.'

THUD.

'Oh.'

Sockball clasps his hands and points them ahead of him, at an empty point on the wall above his socks.

'Take a tree,' Sockball says, 'take two trees next to each other, put them on television and it's boring; see them in the park and … well, not quite so boring, is it?' His hands are now waving to the sides, like an airhostess pointing to the exits. 'You can walk in between them, or around them, or you can look at them from an angle of your choosing.'

THUD.

He picks up his socks.

Revelation

Sockball isn't a friend – he doesn't have a list on him – he's a neighbour. Adam doesn't know anything about him: not his birthday, not his girlfriend's birthday, not even if there is a girlfriend.

THUD.

So he's safe. This is safe. Although, today, his neighbour is more probing than normal: Sockball is asking questions.

'So what's your favourite place to be Alastair Sim?' says Sockball, bending down to pick up his ball of socks.

That's an easy question to answer.

'I don't have one.' He does indeed have one but he'll keep that information to himself.

'At the end of the corridor, by the stairs?' Sockball guesses correctly.

Very recently, people have been able to see through him. His mind is readable: even the most obscure things about him are known by people with whom he has little history – Sockball and Yvette, that is. To tell you the truth, it's quite a relief, once you get used to it. There's nothing to fake, to hide about yourself. It frees up a lot of mind space to think about other matters. He supposes if you're the sort of person who doesn't hide that your favourite game is sock-ball, you're also the sort of person who doesn't mind other people impersonating Alastair Sim.

'Yes, the stairs, it's a good place.'

'Yes? Why's that?'

'I don't know, something about the light.'

'I understand,' says Sockball, as if he does.

He thinks more about it as he watches Sockball play sock-ball.

THUD.

He likes the way the mood on the stairs changes throughout the day. In the morning it's bright and optimistic, yellow light floods the landing and the bottom of the stairs in a pool of positivity. Leaving the building on a sunny morning puts him in a good mood. He's an altogether nicer man to be around.

THUD. 'Strike one.'

The atmosphere in the evening is altogether darker and more sinister, and there's very little you can do about it. You just have to go along with it and join in. There's no point being a comedic Alastair Sim if the set is sinister – it doesn't work. You have to be a sinister Alastair Sim. Or a nervous one. You need to creep up the stairs very carefully, as if you're trying not to disturb anybody – creep lightly, evenly distribute your weight as you move up one step at a time, wincing occasionally for extra effect. It's a complicated business but can be rewarding.

THUD. 'Strike two.'

Only two weeks ago, before his interest in Alastair Sim, he had replaced a flickering lightbulb and its fitting. How the damage was caused is a mystery, given it was so far out of harm's way (he'd had to use a tall stepladder to get to it). My word, what would he give for that now: an atmospheric effect he'd pay for: Hitchcockian in suspense, worthy of the best black and white thriller. A perfect setting?

THUD. 'Strike three.'

They are disturbed by a knock on the door; they turn to look at it – Adam on the sofa, Sockball bending over to pick up his socks – both expecting somebody to enter, but nobody does. It isn't open.

Opening the door, Sockball is greeted with a kiss (on the cheek), followed by the words, 'Hi, Luke.'

It's a familiar voice this woman has. A woman who obviously knows Sockball well. Well enough to know his real name isn't Sockball. A woman who could not have known Sockball already had a guest. A woman who joins Adam on the couch and gives him, too, a kiss (on the cheek).

'Hi, Adam,' she says, the woman: Yvette.

'Hi,' Adam says, containing his hurt, his face revealing no emotion.

The fact that Yvette knows so much about him, he likes and does not question. But he'd imagined she was like this with him only. That her knowledge about everything he does has a pleasant, obvious reason, which he is not yet aware of, and is a result of her infatuation with him. The notion that Yvette knows everything about everybody had not occurred to him.

Adam has never asked Sockball his real name. He called him Sockball on the first evening they'd met, when he'd been asked if he'd like to take off his socks and throw them at the wall. The name just stuck.

This had worked. There was a link between knowing a name and knowing everything else about that person. The rules in his new life allowed for a neighbour and a lover. No friends as such, no unwanted time consumption at least. And now, without thinking, Yvette has called his neighbour by his actual name.

'Want to play?' Sockball asks Yvette.

She takes this as an offer, pulls off her tights and joins 'Luke', as she calls him, in a game.

THUD. Thud.

She doesn't put much effort into her throwing, but has remarkable accuracy.

THUD. Thud.

Of course, the second thud, her thud, is less noisy, probably because her tights aren't as heavy. Adam's about to ask them to swap throwing objects – to test this theory – when he realises he's lost interest.

'You want to try?' Yvette asks, hitching her skirt up and squatting, evidently as part of some pre-throwing ritual.

'No.'

THUD. Thud.

Sock-ball is a better game with more throwers. It's more fluid and there's less walking involved. Apparently, game etiquette dictates that turns are taken in picking up the objects (socks, and now tights) from the floor and passing them back to their throwers.

The throwing is synchronised out of habit rather than design: they look like they've thrown a thousand socks together. Occasionally, after throwing, they even smile in unison.

'It's a much better game played here than in the hallway or on the stairs,' she tells him, winding up her throwing arm and squatting before pelting the wall.

THUD. Thud.

Mystery of the damaged light fitting solved.

Very soon it becomes apparent that Sockball and Yvette had once dated. They too had been lovers – a romance which had finished some time ago, yet they are still on first-name terms. Cheek-kissing terms too.

The jealousy Adam feels surprises him.

11

The Final Push

At work, a commotion: brazenly, with little thought for his feelings, the office organises a Christmas party and invites him. How is he supposed to feel? Delighted at such an opportunity to converse with strangers?

Hasn't he got enough to contend with, what with people approaching him at work at every opportunity?

And it's only October.

And this is just the beginning.

There are bound to be more events. It's not the only invitation he will receive. There's bound to be an office outing too.

Then there's Christmas television. A lot of whingeing to avoid, about how there's nothing good on at Christmas any more, followed by: 'Did you see' blah blah 'the Christmas Special?' Blah blah blah blah. 'Good, wasn't it?'

Filling in his morning spreadsheet (a low swear-word tally today), Adam wonders whether the extra bitterness he feels towards Christmas has anything to do with recent revelations.

In the café he notices a change to his coffee. The toppings are getting bigger. The chocolate on his cappuccino consists of more than just the grated kind: there are heavy-looking cubes too suspended in the foam, along with raspberries and cinnamon and large pecans, and syrup.

He pokes around with his spoon, underneath the cubes, to see if they are getting any extra support. Clearly they are not.

Watching them dissolve into froth, he looks more closely at them: there are no bubble holes. The blocks, he concludes are solid.

It's not just the coffee: the atmosphere in the café is suspicious too. The silence today is in a good mood, punctuated as it is with sounds of coffee gratification. It's most normal for the café – the *mmms* and *ahhhs* of satisfied customers – but the atmosphere he's noticed is odd.

It's quiet. People are talking. But not as often as you'd expect. There's not a lot of noise for a café this populated: it's not in proportion – the noise level and the customer count. It's as if he was watching a film with the sound down. There's the occasional giggle: people are laughing, enjoying themselves; right now he can see more than fifty diners, but if he were to close his eyes and listen – he closes his eyes and listens: it feels like there are no more than ten in the café; a stop-off on the way to a convention for the timid; the noise of ten quiet people, less maybe, if not for the slurping and the munching. Of course, yes, people talk, there is a quiet hum of communication, but that's it.

Has there been a subtle change in atmosphere, or is he just more aware? Either way, he'll be paying closer attention to the environment from now on.

Opening his eyes, he finds Yvette sitting across the table, staring at him intently.

They do not talk about her past with his sock-throwing neighbour. Instead they focus on the matter in hand: preparing for their afternoon of canvassing.

They talk about the climate. They agree, after consulting the weather forecasts in various papers, that on their afternoon expedition it would be wise to wear some kind of waterproof clothing: in the event of a deluge, this would free Adam up from his umbrella-holding duties, allowing him to be more proactive in their canvassing pitch.

'With only one day more to go before the *Monsoon Wedding* screening it is imperative that all our energies are focused on persuading more people to come,' she tells him in earnest, as if he wasn't aware of the gravity of the situation.

'I am aware of the gravity of the situation,' Adam tells her without a trace of irritation. Yes, the situation is precarious for both of them. Adam's new life has been founded on trips to the cinema. Yvette's history was too: not only did her parents meet in that cinema, she tells him, but she was conceived there too – a fact she found cringe-worthy while her parents were alive, so much so that she avoided Screen Seven for many years; but since they had passed away, the screening room had gained a greater significance. Yvette tells him she had visited the cinema on the day of her parents' funeral, had gone to Screen Seven after the wake because they'd talked about the place so often, because it was the place that made them happiest, and for once she wanted to see why. She had watched a film called Run Lola Run, the first non-mainstream film she had ever seen, and from that day she was hooked.

He feels slightly perturbed at his selfishness. Until now,

he'd rarely thought about Yvette's plight, preferring instead to dwell on the injustices that closing the programme would heap upon his own life. It hadn't occurred to him that she too had an important reason to embark upon their mammoth undertaking.

'I am aware of the gravity of the situation,' Adam tells her again, this time meaning it.

He clasps her hand.

'It'll be OK,' he whispers.

Her breathing slows.

She smiles at him. They drink their coffees in silence, looking at each other, the emotional distress of the last few moments cushioned by *mmms* and *ahhhs* of contentment from their fellow diners. It's a silence that stirs Adam's sense of urgency in their afternoon of marketing ahead: one day to go, one last push for attendees. It's time to get serious.

He talks about Yvette's canvassing performance and suggests that they could pitch more people if they shortened the dance routine in her third act.

She leans across the table and calls him something, invents a cute name for him – quite complimentary and a little rude – then sits back in her chair, smiles and waits for reciprocation.

The Conversation

The taste of orange snap biscuits permeates Sockball's flat. His potpourri really does smell like biscuits. Adam will have to ask him where he gets it from. In the past he's made judgements about people who use potpourri, but now they're making a version with a biscuit scent, he thinks he might get some.

While tree-watching – the blackbirds are nowhere to be seen, and anyway, Adam suspects that while Sockball is interested in all nature, he has a particular fondness for trees – they do not talk about Yvette and Sockball having dated.

Adam is a little hurt by this. Almost as if he expects an apology.

'Don't they inflate their chests?' asks Sockball, breaking Adam from a zone-out.

'What?'

'When they're trying to attract a mate, they inflate their chests, don't they? And their necks?'

'Why, yes, they do.' Sockball has made a good point. It's obviously a subject he's been giving some consideration.

'Well, maybe it's good at that. It could be bad at chirping, but good at body-inflation.'

This is very true. The blackbird would have a limited range in which to impress a companion, but at close range its bloated body may be very engaging to another blackbird.

'Is it doing it now?' Adam asks.

'I don't know.'

Adam glances at his watch: It's too early for the bird; the thing doesn't usually appear for a couple of hours.

'I don't think it's awake yet.'

Again they find themselves looking at the Chilean. Another early morning spent tree-watching.

A Weekend Break

The momentum of television avoidance is with him: three weeks he has been without it (with four or five exceptions), but now he finds both opportunity and motive on his landing.

Sockball is going away on a conference – something to do with the rubber business, or textiles, he can't remember – and has asked him to water his plants. Oh, he could decline – but what if he needs a favour in return, what if it is he who needs his plants watering, or his goldfish fed? It is a delicate matter – Charlie the goldfish has a sensitive stomach and doesn't like strangers. OK, so he could ask Yvette, but what if she decides to be with him on this holiday he'd be taking, what then?

No. He'll agree to it.

'I agree – to water your plants,' he says.

'Good,' replies Sockball.

'Just move them into my apartment before you leave.' Adam can't trust himself with unsupervised access to a television that is not set up with an adequate security system.

'Unless you possess some green fabric, a set of yellow post-it notes and a goldfish?'

Recreating his own television-avoidance system in Sockball's apartment would be a straightforward task.

Sockball merely asks for time to ponder the choice he has been given, then closes his apartment door. He does not offer Adam tea and biscuits, or any form of refreshment while the decision is being thought over. Adam is left standing in the corridor outside Sockball's flat.

A few moments earlier, Adam had been pacing and muttering as he'd passed Sockball's door, as Alastair Sim, when the door had opened and he had been accosted. Adam had hoped a jovial Alastair Sim would put him in a good mood for the task ahead of him today: the film screening that he and Yvette had worked so hard to save was a mere two hours away, and Adam had hoped a brief jolly Alastair Sim might make him less grumpy about proceedings. Yes, he needs to save the screening programme, but that means *people*, sitting in his screening room, an event that would normally send him bananas.

Only a few hours ago, Adam had been watching trees with Sockball. Now he's standing in the hallway outside the fellow's flat while the man is deliberating whether to set up a television-avoidance system in his own flat or just give Adam his plants to look after while he goes on an absurd weekend conference.

After a short while, the door opens and Sockball passes Adam several large plants, which Adam, one by one, takes to his apartment, placing them in the kitchen.

Monsoon Wedding

As the lights in the cinema dim, the pattern on the ceiling above him disappears into the darkness. By the time he's lost all perception of ceiling, the cinema has eight customers: Mr Geoff Porter; the Cat Man (the guy he'd helped search for his cat); two more couples they'd conversed with on their campaign (whose names have escaped him); Yvette, and himself.

Of course, he can't see Yvette – once you've lost all perception of ceiling, you lose all perception of back. And as she likes to come in near the start of a film, when it's pitch black, and sit at the back, Adam can't be sure she is there.

They had agreed to sit in their comfort positions for this screening. Sitting with Yvette at the back, knowing there would be masses of people ahead would, he thought, be too stressful. Sitting at the front in denial, for him, is more palatable.

Denial, though, is difficult when the first man to arrive, the Cat Man, had noticed Adam, slapped him on the back and shouted, 'Alright, geeza.' The nerve of the man: first he informs the police of a fictitious catnapping crime, pointing his finger squarely at Adam, and then he disturbs his sense of reality in his sanctuary, Screen Seven! Since the Cat Man's arrival, Adam's ears have become overly sensitive.

Suddenly, it strikes him that he has no idea how many customers they need to save the programme. Is eight enough? If there were eight for every screening in this screen, would that be enough?

It is conceivable there are more than eight customers, though; he has no idea how many may be hiding at the back with Yvette, in the dark: the dimming of the lighting may lend a certain atmosphere to the proceedings but makes a head-count more difficult and adds stress to the proceedings: he has consumed two coffees, three chocolate flakes, and the film is yet to begin.

For the past five minutes he has been watching the entrance, glancing occasionally on hearing the doors close – it's not something he is used to: glancing at doors, hoping more people will invade his space.

It'd be much easier to do a head-count from the back, where late arrivals are easily spotted, silhouetted by the backdrop of the screen.

When the film finishes he raises this issue with Yvette. Clearly he has been given the wrong task on this occasion.

'Surely it would have been easier for you to do a head-count,' he tells her, standing in the aisle of the still-dark screening room.

'You can do a head-count now, can't you!' she says, to his mind rather pointlessly.

'There are only two of us.'

'There are others in the foyer, they've just left; you could count those too, before they leave.'

Making haste to the foyer, they find the box office, which is constructed mainly from Perspex, is being attacked with large stick-like objects and yellow jelly babies.

The couple holding the sticks are arguing with box-office staff, shouting obscenities in time to the beat of stick against window, while a voice emanating from behind the window screams, 'No refunds.'

The window buckles.

Feeling a small amount of responsibility for the situation and the plight of the box-office assistants, Adam and Yvette stay in the foyer to keep an eye on events while they chat.

After consultation, they agree it would not be the right time to converse with the owner of the cinema about reinstating the Screen Seven programme and agree to approach him next Monday at midday.

Their consultation is disturbed by a stray sherbet lemon, which skids on the floor between them, bouncing against the frame of the exit door with a metallic twang.

The Stick Couple are now in confectionery throwing boiled sweets and popcorn.

The box-office assistants take the opportunity to make their escape, pushing past Adam and Yvette through the exit doors.

Adam and Yvette follow.

As they head off in the direction of the patisserie, they're halted by a loud slamming noise. Turning, they observe Mr Geoff Porter running directly at them, the cinema's swing doors flapping behind him.

The man, obviously unaware of the correct stopping distance associated with legs travelling at high speed, skids to a halt two metres past them; he would have gone through them if they hadn't in unison turned sideways creating the gap through which he had passed.

To their surprise, the man offers to help them out: deliver leaflets, pitch door to door, get them refreshments when needed.

Yvette accepts his offer of help and will later thank him with a free coffee.

12

The Letter

Adam finds himself, yet again, in a position where he waits for water to boil before embarking on a matter of some urgency: reading his letter. He'd found it on his doorstep this morning, tied to a packet of HobNobs, the plain biscuit variety.

Over a cup of tea and several of the biscuits, he reads it. When finished reading, he reads it again and finishes the rest of his now cold tea. The letter is folded neatly and placed in a drawer built into the kitchen table – where he keeps his notes and lists.

It is, he thinks, a little too blunt, but he admires its clarity, her clarity: she has left little room for confusion. It is over. It clearly says so in the first line, and the last paragraph. It's a very harsh letter.

In it, she makes a few very good points. It does not surprise him that she knows so much about him. He's used to it. But she lists many of the character flaws he thought he'd discarded with his old life along with his unwanted possessions and ex-friends he no longer identifies with. Character flaws – he thinks about this seriously – are obviously a lot harder to discard than he'd thought: they are aware of where he lives, and once discarded seem to have found their own way back to his personality. So much so, that many of the issues she talks about he thought no longer existed.

This is an occasion in which the appropriate course of action would be to dwell on her negative points: HE ABSOLUTELY WILL NOT DO IT.

———

He takes a new route to work: a path that coincidentally, and rather, for him, disappointingly, leaves him standing at the Silk Street traffic lights at eight fifty-five; exactly the same time as the previous day; exactly the same time as every other day he's worked there.

It's the third new route this week. Standing at the traffic lights (now at eight fifty-six), he retraces his steps: the walk this morning to work had included a circuit of a small park – paced as himself (being Alastair Sim has for some reason momentarily lost its appeal). He'd also stopped at a bakery for a rather good and now half-finished fresh coffee. While drinking the coffee, he'd prematurely eaten his banana and had to stop off at the fruit shop for a replacement. He'd expected the excursions to add ten minutes to his journey.

Out of habit he glances towards the patisserie, then continues to work as normal.

While The Boss debriefs him on something or other (probably the cost of office biros), he successfully manages not to take in any information at all except a guess-how-much count of zero and a swear count of sixteen. He does, though, spend the time unwisely looking out of the window.

Over the last few weeks, what with having to save the Screen Seven programme, he's been fading out on The Boss more than normal, leaving the meetings with little more than a swear count. The guess-how-much game has been abandoned completely in the pursuit of a higher swear-word tally.

At lunch he rereads her letter – it's not quite as eloquent as he first thought. The first two pages are well written, yes, as is the last paragraph, but the intermediate seven pages are plain babble. First she tells him it is over. Then, during the babble, she talks of a six-month sabbatical. Finally, she concludes by telling him that it's over, and that the biscuits to which the letter was attached are a goodbye gift.

With the rest of the day he does nothing. Sometimes he does nothing as himself, sometimes as Alastair Sim. He does nothing at work. He does nothing at home. Then, in a frenzy of activity he pulls the green fabric off the television set, peels post-it notes from the screen and slaps them aggressively (but neatly) onto the arm of the sofa. Every third note he reads: 'Don't watch me', 'Turn me off', 'You hate television', 'Water Sockball's Plants', 'Read a book', 'Buy more post-it notes', 'Dump friends'.

By the time he's finished reading the notes it's midnight. He knows *Late Night Poker* is about to begin but television too, it seems, has lost its appeal.

He goes to bed early.

Sleepless in Suburbia

The pain he's in is physical and getting worse. A kind of growling pain emanates from his intestines. He peers down at the general area. It gargles.

Also, the blackbird is screeching.

He looks at his clock – it's two a.m.

They weren't planning on seeing each other for a few days anyway. She's busy, away for a long weekend at a coffee conference. He wouldn't have seen her today. So he's not sure if the pain he's feeling is because he's been dumped or because she's away on business – just a plain, though rather wimpish pain of missing somebody.

Technically, the pain of being dumped shouldn't start until Monday – the next time they'd arranged to meet, a meeting they'd scheduled with the Cinema Owner for midday. It's another matter which she appears to have overlooked – ownership of their campaign. Does she expect him to sit at home suddenly not caring what happens to Screen Seven?

Adam clambers out of bed and makes his way to the kitchen, where he stares at the Chilean while munching HobNobs (the plain biscuit variety).

'I'm leaving town,' she'd typed. A rather dramatic turn of phrase, followed by another: 'So don't come after me.' Equally dramatic, and a little cliché. Come after her? Why would he? The phrase implies he's some kind of psychotic madman. Sitting back in his chair, he mutters the phrase to himself: 'Come after her. Come after her.' He varies the tone, rocking back and forth, adding some Alastair Sim subtext, then shakes his head: it's just not him. It does not reflect his sensitive side.

Besides, where would he start? Where would she stay besides her apartment? The only contact they share is Sockball, and he lives in Adam's building. That's hardly escaping his evil clutches, as she so clearly implies. And it's not 'leaving town'.

The subtopics so clearly typed in capital letters are another source of discomfort: 'IT IS OVER'; 'DO NOT CALL'; 'DO NOT VISIT'; 'PROBLEMS WITH ADAM'. A most negative letter.

It's a letter which appears to get more negative every time he reads it.

In an effort to be upbeat about the matter, he paces the hallway as Alastair Sim while wearing a Hawaiian shirt. It has a steadying effect, and by the time he returns to the kitchen table he's calm enough to resume his bird-watching activity.

While looking at the Chilean, he reminisces: thinks about her bad points, about how she'd sneak up on him, creep behind the sofa every time he dunked a bourbon cream, then bite it from between his fingers. To the casual observer this action could seem cute, the soggy crumbs left betwixt finger and thumb a sign of affection. BUT TEN BISCUITS IN A ROW? It's most inconsiderate. Theft is what he calls it.

And it's not just the bourbon creams, there's the tea to consider too – that many dunked biscuits and half a mug is lost. The stresses that woman placed upon his being were exorbitant. No wonder the note had been tied to a packet of HobNobs; what guilt she must have felt.

Later, he'll add it to her list. In red ink, in the column marked 'NEGATIVES', he'll write the words 'Biscuit Rustler'. It will do little to shift his mood.

The blackbird snaps him from zone-out. Seeing it, he checks for signs of chest inflation – Sockball has given him binoculars with his plants, and he uses them now to spy on his feathered friend.

Its chest is a little small, but he supposes that as there are no females in the vicinity, that's OK.

Then he remembers that birds strut. They dance. It's another way of attracting a companion. They chirp; they inflate their chests; and they dance. That's three ways, at least.

Could the poor little thing be a good dancer? He looks at it: it's not attempting to inflate its body, it's not puffing up, and it's not strutting. Just chirping, out of tune.

And for a moment Adam admires it. It's not even trying to be something it's not. It's not trying to be bigger than it is, or to impress with its strutting when it's not in its character. It's just being itself. And loudly. Potential mates either like it or they don't – they want it, or it's an evolutionary dead end. The bird accepts this, and so must he.

Yvette doesn't want him. She isn't going to get in contact. She doesn't want his company. She has given her reasons – he looks at her letter, page nine, the final line, it reads:

I don't fancy you – it's a chemical thing.

The Art of Listening

At his desk this morning while eating his banana, he had reread her letter. It's very surprising she does not refer to his use of the word '*date*'; it's the only thing they argued about. 'You use the word "*date*" like some people use the word "*and*",' she'd told him, quite clearly, on a number of occasions. A bit of an exaggeration, he had thought at the time, and had let it pass. But her letter fails to mention it.

It does, though, mention other character flaws. Number one, for example, is that he does not listen. How true. A point that he cannot fault, considering he's thinking about this while his boss is in mid-conversation and he has no idea what the man is blathering on about.

This trait of not focusing on what is being said, he had considered to be one of his most positive attributes, but he was not aware that it had crept into his communications with Yvette. Yes, he zoned out on his neighbour Sockball and his ex-friends, and the fruit shop owner, and the bus driver. But with Yvette?

If he was the sort of man who listened, maybe he would be the sort of man who could see. Had he opened his eyes he would have seen Yvette sitting behind him at the back of the cinema; would have noticed her walking down his corridor to visit Sockball; would have noticed they work within polite shouting distance of each other.

Lunchtime, in a bookshop, he browses the self-help section. With several promising-looking books, he relocates to the shop's coffee bar.

He finds out that women, apparently, like men to listen – something he could have deduced for himself. Reading the obvious induces a pang of anger. Blood boils. Biscuits are munched. Tea is gulped. Anger subsides.

He reads on.

He reads that 'listening is about MORE than actually listening', then that 'listening is ONLY about listening'. Another pang. Another garibaldi. Same coffee.

He skims several more books, then gives up.

Zoning out had helped him out of some difficult situations in the past. Not paying attention at some key moments had helped him survive his ex-friends and secured him his job. But when conversing with Yvette, he wants actually to hear what's being said. Honestly. Even if it's not in the acknowledging, sympathetic, responsive way they write about in those self-help books, even if it's just in the standard hearing sense of the word, he wants to listen.

He is going to attempt to cure his wandering, lazy mind. Oh, he's aware of the downside: it means he'll be less able to turn to this skill when he needs it. He'll have to put up with that infernal brain pollution people far too often attack him with. But it may be worth the cost.

Supermarket

The cupboard is bare, the last tin of corned beef gone, fried and eaten with his last onion (the Ryvita crispbreads were gone long ago). He walks to the supermarket.

Rolling past the fruit and veg with his trolley, he notices that pomegranates are in season. He buys several, along with a large spray can of cream, using them as soon as he gets home to invent a new type of coffee – a lucky dip cappuccino. You take a standard coffee, add a thin layer of sprayed cream, several pomegranate seeds, and cover with a thicker layer of cream-and-cocoa topping.

It's a great cappuccino, with a surprise that lurks beneath the surface. He makes two, one with a pomegranate surprise, the other with submerged bananas, then closes his eyes, switches them around several times, and sips.

'Ahhh …'

He has always disliked fairytale endings. He's not talking here about the final act of a story, no, but the words 'and they lived happily ever after', the bit after the end of a film when everything has been resolved. Sounds a little dull, living happily ever after. After all, the reason he likes a film is the conflict, the tension, the twists and turns. But when you get to happy ever after, the twists have finished, haven't they? So where does that leave you? Being bored, he supposes. That's the problem with him and Yvette as a couple. They were already living 'happily ever after' when they met. There was just not enough conflict in their relationship. They agreed on too much.

And that's the good thing about his friends: they're always irritating; there's something to get involved in.

He's feeling proud of himself – of his ability to put such life-turmoil into perspective – when a memory hits him. He walks over to his kitchen-table drawer and retrieves her list. He is about to write something in the positive column when he sees it's already there: that *'she knows about film'*. It's the seventh positive on her list, underneath positive number five – that *'she knows things'* – and positive six – that *'she prompts him in a good way'*. He looks down the sheet, scanning positive after positive, turns the page, and the next one, and another, and counts the total: seventy-eight positives so far.

Strange how he appreciates things when they're gone. This comforts him: if he was still with her, or rather if she was with him, he feels sure she would not have amassed such a large tally. No. Probably only forty or fifty plusses; and she would have more negatives too. He flicks back to the front sheet and counts negatives. There are three so far. He strains to think of a fourth to add to the list. Thinks about the small differences, reasons they might not get along. After half an hour he adds to her tally:

NEGATIVE NUMBER 4: Banana is not one of her
favourite fruits, not in her top five.

He strains again for another negative, a negative characteristic he himself does not possess. The problem is they are too similar.

For some, this would be the downside, being too similar to your partner: there would be little new news or points of view to spark a conversation. But even this has an upside: it makes it easier to be himself. It doesn't spoil his plan of being a loner; it's as if he's on his own *and* with somebody else.

He turns over several pages and appends it to her positives:

NUMBER 79: Similar to me.

Pace. Mutter. Sit. 'Yes, inspector.'

A lap of the table, and it becomes clear to him that he needs not to add to her negative qualities but to look more closely at her positives. She has too many – like on page one:

NUMBER 1: Like the way she
pronounces 'cappuccino'.

Sounds like the ramblings of a lovesick teenager: he deletes it and pauses. Yes, he does like the way she pronounces 'cappuccino' but there are other words she uses which are much more appealing.

When they're in bed, for instance, the way she uses the word 'lovely' – he should incorporate that into her list of positives. Only, he is uneasy about letting secrets out of the bedroom, even if they only travel as far as his kitchen notepad – a woman's integrity needs to be preserved, and papers held in kitchen drawers, once found, could be circulated to all and sundry.

Only this morning he'd read about a private email of a sexual nature which had ended up being circulated to several hundred thousand world-wide.

While taking refreshments, feeding Charlie the goldfish and looking through the bedroom window for the blackbird, he thinks of hypothetical situations in which a stranger would stumble across his information and put it on the internet. The possibilities are endless.

Pace. Mutter. Sit. 'Yes, inspector.'

Another circuit of the kitchen.

Deciding to be cryptic about her bedroom secret, he scribbles:

NUMBER 80: BS-Lovely

It's a solution, he notes, he'd arrived at some time ago: number three on her list reads: 'BS-Sexy'.

The theme tune to *The Godfather* rings through the wall from the flat of High-Pitched Squeak Man. It has an echoey quality to it, as if it's being watched in the bathroom. It reminds him of his ex-friends – their obsession with trying to be somebody they're not.

In those films, if you're in the group, you're family. And once you're family, you stay family. There is no escape. It's about honour and respect.

The way he had handled ridding himself of his ex-friends – could they have felt this way: betrayed, depressed, hurt? A feeling of wanting to throw up; hungry, self-pitying, tired?

It's always easier to remember those occasions when you could have been kinder, less self-important if only you'd thought about consequences, been less wrapped up in your own issues. What did he say in his goodbye speech in the pub that day? He can't remember.

From the table drawer he seizes the letters and the lists – all of them – and rips them up, one by one, tearing them in halves, then quarters, then eighths, laughing, attempting to turn into the madman she insinuates he is.

Lists on friends, lists on lovers. Gone.

It may well be the case that the blackbird's sole goal is the acquisition of a partner, but it's not one of Adam's goals. The whole meeting Yvette saga has been a distraction from his big plan – a distraction which has, in various guises, soaked up all his spare time recently. The acquisition of a mate may be a goal if you're covered in feathers; Adam, however, has much more pressing things on his mind.

13

The Wedding

A bit of an ordeal you'd think, but it has its upside: it hadn't cost him anything, the transport was free and he'd been allowed to sit – with adequate restraints – in the back of the car this time, rather than the boot. They'd also purchased and wrapped, on his behalf, a wedding gift, saving him time and more money. Also, he'd not had to go to a suit fitting, though the costume they provided he'd rather not think about: quite an understandable precaution from their point of view; still, vulgar in the extreme on such an occasion. He is surprised the bride and groom had put up with it, aware as he is of the importance placed on these occasions traditionally by the happy couple.

Certainly he had provided a point of interest: their wedding photographs, no doubt, will provide a great deal of amusement.

Steven, the best man, had instigated the deed, he is sure. They'd had no direct conversation throughout the day and even now, on the drive back home, he remains quiet, and, Adam senses, a little angry. Jay has also adopted the silent approach, though has stopped short of ignoring Adam completely – from the passenger seat, Jay has been glancing over his shoulder at him for the past five minutes.

Earlier, at the wedding, the mood had been lighter. The reaction he had received had been mostly welcoming: there had been little hostility shown, and they had removed his gag so that he could partake in the dining.

He had shown restraint in the face of verbal derision, declining both the wine thrust upon him during the meal and the champagne toast to the bride and groom.

The main thrust of conversation was a concoction of stories reminiscing about how drunk they'd got on various occasions.

'It's a laugh, isn't it?' his ex-friend Steven had said in conclusion to every story, in an accent trying to be New York mafia.

Though his accent was passable, his choice of words, in Adam's opinion, lacked mafia credibility. The rest of the group appeared to disagree: Steven's stock phrase was well received; Jay, in particular, coughed a laugh each time he heard it.

The rest of the occasion was fun and touching and sad: at one point, while most people were up dancing, Jay had approached him. 'You're the only one in this group I can stand, besides Karen,' he'd said, and then had stroked Adam's shoulder.

Now, somewhere on the motorway, the mood is frosty. Neither Jay nor Steven have spoken to him or to each other on the return journey so far. It's a moody, aggressive silence that lasts until they're halfway home.

'We are nice, for fuck sake,' Steven spurts. 'We socialise. We buy each other thoughtful gifts. We are good people –

we are normal. We like a drink.'

Adam's glad, now, that they'd re-gagged him after dinner.

They *like a drink*. How could he not like a man who *likes a drink*? It's been a horrible mistake, taking a break from people who like a drink – why would he want to do that? Perhaps because he has a liver problem! Perhaps because, although it's not a life-threatening condition, he wanted to follow his doctor's advice and drink less? Perhaps because he's fed up of constant mild hangovers that sap days from his life, getting in the way of his search for something bigger in his life, something deeper, something with meaning.

There's a lengthy silence as they drive another ten miles along the motorway through torrential rain, a silence which is broken when they pull into a service station.

Jay gets out of the car and fills the tank.

'We do this for your own good,' Steven says. 'Look, either you don't want us, which means there's something wrong with us, OR you are abnormal. And there can't be anything wrong with us. NOT ALL OF US. NOT COLLECTIVELY. You may not like Karen when she's rude, or Jay when he whinges on about money, but there can't be something wrong with all of us can there?'

Jay returns from the service till after paying for petrol. An argument breaks out over why he hadn't purchased some snacks while he was at the counter. 'It's implicit, expected, isn't it,' Steven says, 'that if you're buying petrol, you buy group snacks while you're at it.'

Jay attempts to defend himself: 'Why the fuck don't you pay for the petrol then? It's your car.'

After a brief heated discussion on car passenger etiquette and taxi fares from the middle of the motorway, things go eerily quiet. The three of them sit in silence, in a motionless car, in the petrol station, for five minutes. After which time, a compromise is struck: Steven goes for snacks, Jay agrees to pay for them upon his return.

While Steven is away, Jay looks at Adam in the rear-view mirror: 'I think you're suffering from low self-esteem,' Jay says.

Adam shakes his head.

'I think you are.'

Adam shakes his head faster and harder.

'I knew you'd say that.'

Adam gives up.

The service station is surprisingly empty. The rain eases up. Steven makes his way to the car carrying two large paper bags of food.

'You don't want to hang with us because you've got low self-esteem,' Jay says quickly, one last time before the snacks arrive.

Two large hamburgers, two medium fries, two apple pies, one portion of onion rings and a magazine.

Jay huffs his disapproval. Then pays for everything, except the magazine.

'How about spirits? You can drink spirits, can't you? It's just beer that's the problem.' Steven looks at Adam through the rear-view mirror while unwrapping a burger.

Adam shakes his head.

'What about wine? You can drink wine.'

Adam shakes his head again.

'No. You can drink wine. You're not an old woman, you're in your early thirties, for fuck sake.' Steven takes a large aggressive bite of hamburger and spends a lot of energy trying to swallow it before running through a list of beverages of varying alcoholic content.

It's not just about their intolerance of teetotallers. They are working under the misapprehension that if they can find a suitable alcoholic beverage he can tolerate – one which boosts his liver and leaves him hangover free – he'll rejoin their little gang. But there are many more things on his lists. Many more negatives. He thought that had been made clear. Really he'd like to just show them the lists – they could see their own problems, work on them in their spare time, and turn up fixed.

Or he could just be more assertive.

'So, wine – really it's just rotting fruit isn't it? If you can drink grape juice, you can drink wine, can't you?' They both turn to look at him. 'Can you drink grape juice?'

An argument ensues as to whether Adam should drink whisky or wine. Steven says Adam can drink wine; Jay – still seething about the magazine he was asked to purchase – says he can drink whisky; they end up, both looking at him, suggesting a wine-whisky cocktail compromise.

Really it's time they started to have children. Stop them talking to grown-ups like one. This is what Adam's turning into: a surrogate child. His attempts to be diplomatic about this whole leaving his past thing, his plan to let the course of events just play out, appear not to be working. Another plan is needed. A plan he can be more aggressive with.

Somehow boundaries have been broken. He's not able to pull himself away from this little charade. He's not being assertive enough, not making it clear that he really wants to break things off.

He knows there are benefits to having friends – something to do with having somebody help him save Screen Seven. And that friends are supposed to have a big advantage over family: you're able to choose them. But this means you can also choose not to have them.

Sensing that their speeches are having little impact, Jay and Steven ignore him and talk among themselves, a conversation about industry:

'I'm thinking about going into the meat-packing business,' Steven says to Jay, halfway through his second portion of fries.

'Really?' Jay nods.

'Or the restaurant business.'

'Really.' Jay's still nodding. 'Well, you do know a lot about food.'

'Italian food. Pasta …' Steven struggles to think of another Italian food. 'Pasta mainly. Lots of sauces.'

'Meat-packing?'

'Yeah, well, frozen chicken.'

'Or casinos. I may open a casino.'

Simultaneously they laugh, and start quoting lines from the film *Casino*.

Of course, it is easier to go along with the abduction now he's alone. Really alone. Now there's no Yvette and no Sockball – people that were never part of his big plan anyway.

At two minutes past three in the morning Adam is dumped in a motorway lay-by. They do have the decency to untie him, making it much easier, this time, to hitch a lift the rest of the way home.

Life's a Film

The wedding reception had finished early – after a fight had broken out on the dance floor – and it's still early when they drop him off.

Adam stops at a late-night greasy spoon on the way home: watching his ex-friends eat burgers and chips has given him an appetite for grease.

He orders an all-day English breakfast and a mug of tea, which he drinks while reading the newspaper supplements.

What rubbish they print in these magazines these days, Adam thinks, while reading an article about film and writing. It claims that most problems in life have been written about. Life, it appears, is very much like a film. Somebody somewhere has probably made a film about what he's going through right now, or written a novel. If this were true, all he'd need to do is find a copy and watch (or read) the ending. The film may or may not be starring Alastair Sim. This is very important.

This theory has one very large hole, a flaw that isn't mentioned until the last paragraph: it only works if there are an infinite number of films. And there aren't. And if there were it would take an awfully long time to find the right one. He'd need help.

Of course, if he went into a video shop and asked for a film about a man who's being kidnapped by his friends and taken to parties and force-fed wedding cake and champagne on pain of … of what, he's not sure … but he is sure they'd think him a lunatic. There may, though, be something in the general area, something related.

He asks at Blockbuster.

'What was the title?'

'No, I'm not sure … Something like, umm, *Honey I've Been Kidnapped and Forced to go to This Wedding.*'

TAP, TAP.

'We've got *My Best Friend's Wedding.*'

He tries the bookshop.

TAP, TAP.

'We've got *How to Win Friends And Influence People.*'

He spends the evening in the self-help section reading a book on guilt.

Jealousy

In his comfy chair, he sits with his green tea, listening to the muffled sound of sock-ball. Something about it bothers him.

THUD.

It's a little late for sock-ball. He looks at his watch – it's midnight. Ten minutes past, in fact.

Thud.

He freezes his whole body mid-gulp, mid-wince, not breathing, not moving, not swallowing, not breathing. Just listening.

THUD. Thud.

Two noises? It's difficult to say, the noises being so muffled.

THUD … Thud.

Definitely two noises: Sockball is playing with Yvette! It's a thought he dismisses immediately; it's very easy to jump to conclusions; any number of reasons could explain the second noise. Sockball may be making the noise himself – closing the fridge door, for example, after releasing his projectile.

THUD. Thud.

But would he have closed the door three times?

THUD. Thud.

Four times?

No, there are two separate pairs of socks hitting the wall, and Sockball never throws more than one pair at a time: that clearly would breach the rules of sock-ball.

Somebody is playing sock-ball with Sockball.

THUD. Thud.

Somebody who is either wearing lightweight socks … Or tights.

He estimates the point of impact, puts his ear to the wall and listens: the only noise he can hear now is the sound of his own breath, a sound that grows louder as worrying thoughts spring at him. So loud is his breathing that it muffles out the sounds from his neighbour's flat. For months he has had superhero hearing, fine-tuned to pick up television programmes at huge distances through walls of neighbours' flats, and now, when there is a much greater need for such a talent, all he can hear is his own stupid loud breath.

Of course, Sockball would be the logical shoulder for Yvette to lean on, he thinks, presupposing she needs a shoulder. The thought cheers him up.

He holds his breath and concentrates:

THUD. Thud.

The noise is clearer.

They're not sleeping with each other, Sockball and Yvette. He's surprised he entertains such a notion.

He bats that thought away and retreats to the kitchen, distracting himself by boiling water. Superpower returned, his sensitive hearing betrays him. Even in the kitchen now he can hear it: the thudding. He listens:

THUD.

He switches the kettle off and checks his watch.

THUD. Thud.

This just will not do. Playing sock-ball at this hour?

Full of rage and jealousy and green tea, he goes to complain.

14

The Spy Who Loves Me

How did this happen? Lunching with an ex-friend now, was he? Karen had turned up on his doorstep unannounced, at one thirty last night, that's how it had begun. And she was crying. And he wasn't there. He was busy being kidnapped (actually he was making his way home after being kidnapped). So she had waited with Sockball and thrown her tights at the wall pretending to be Yvette. (OK, he's not sure about the last bit – she's never actually met Yvette.)

Crying to Sockball, a man she dislikes, she ended up playing sock-ball, a game she dislikes. She was crying still when Adam knocked on the door and asked what Sockball was thinking.

Crying!

The break had been made with his friends – there were still some unresolved issues over the whole abduction thing, but there had been progress. So far, he'd been in contact with those ex-friends twice in a month; against his will, yes, but still an improvement on the multi-weekly torture he'd been enduring over the last few years; unresolved issues, but a marked improvement. Now he's about to eat lunch with one. And why? Because crying women are a weakness of his – a weakness that makes him forget about what he wants and invite them into his home. A sleepless night on his sofa, an argumentative morning, and now they're having lunch!

This will never do.

The woman is messing with his cappuccino. It's a most disturbing occurrence. Karen has taken her spoon and dipped it into his froth. Now, smiling gently at him, maintaining eye contact, she proceeds to eat it, his froth, along with the cocoa powder sprinkled on top: eighty percent of his chocolate covering is gone in one spoonful.

Yes, he does mind.

Part of him, though, is glad he's been saved: after the highs of an Yvette cappuccino, he fears they will never taste the same again. Karen had ordered a cappuccino too, and had stirred her froth and chocolate and three brown sugars immediately into her drink. That was probably her trigger: seeing the fluffy white top of her drink dissolve into her coffee must have been a shock. The grass is always greener, don't they say? She must have thought, Oh fuck, I wish I'd tasted the topping before I'd stirred; and then taken somebody else's.

'Mmmmm. Chocolate,' she says, like she'd never tasted your basic bland cappuccino before. *Have you been on earth long?* he feels like saying. *How was your trip from the land without coffee?*

'I like to drink mine through the froth,' he says. 'It has a mellowing effect on the coffee. You get a mellowed hit from strong coffee, some froth and some chocolate rolling about in your mouth, mixing together, all at the same time.'

He sips his de-frothed cappuccino, thinking he's made his point.

'Shaken, not stirred,' Karen says, laughing. She twitches her nose. 'Mine's too sweet.'

Would Alastair Sim have made a good James Bond? He thinks not. No, not quite Bond; but a great spy. He wants to raise this with her, wants to turn the topic of conversation to a subject of his choosing but knows that he'll have to go into the whole who-is-Alastair-Sim-and-what-films-has-he-been-in saga. Then he knows she'll say, 'Ah, he's the man in those St Trinian's films,' then disagree with him about him being a good spy because that's the only film she remembers him being in; and that would be the end of the discussion. The last time they talked film, she had said she couldn't see the point of watching a black and white film when there are plenty of colour ones around.

A lengthy silence follows while they eat …

He can sit in silence with Yvette; here, though, with Karen, it proves intolerable:

'Alastair Sim would have made a good spy, wouldn't you say?' he inquires.

'Alastair Sim? Yes, he would.'

'Ah.'

Karen finishes her cappuccino quickly, in a single gulp, slamming cup down on top of saucer. Wiping her mouth on her shirt-sleeve, she sighs, relaxing her whole body, then sticks out two fingers at the waitress and wiggles them, ordering two more of the same.

They order sandwiches and rolls as the second set of cappuccinos arrive.

The reason for the crying and her arrival on his doorstep is still a mystery despite Adam's probing into the subject. His line of questioning has centred primarily around her love life – it's not a usual suspect in these circumstances (late-night crying) because there are no usual suspects; it's not something she is prone to, but faced with this new situation, and given the situation in his own love life, he feels he is in a position to provide genuine heartfelt condolence from a position of understanding.

'So what happened with your boyfriend?'

He waits for a reply while Karen scrapes the topping from her new cappuccino and eats it.

'Your boyfriend. You seemed very upset last night.'

She licks her spoon.

'Oh, let's not talk about that now. It's just too upsetting' she says cheerily, then licks her spoon again, suctioning off the last morsel of chocolate.

His previous experience in providing advice about matters of love has been limited; he couldn't describe himself as an agony aunt. Recently the only advice he has given was to a tone-deaf blackbird, and he's not sure if it had been at all constructive or appropriate. He's about to pursue the matter further when he suffers a strong bout of irritability.

Karen dips her well-licked spoon into his chocolate froth and eats it.

Yvette, his ex-girlfriend, may well have been a biscuit rustler, but this is unacceptable. Besides, in Yvette's biscuit rustling he had been an accomplice. Purposely, he'd left his bourbon cream, post-dunking, in mid-air, waiting for it to be engulfed. Yvette's misdemeanour was a sign of affection – erotic too, when he thinks about it. Yvette was giving something: affection, and wet fingers. Karen, however, appears to just like chocolate froth. It doesn't occur to her that he may also like it, that this may be the reason he had ordered it instead of the plain coffee that she has now left him with.

It had been a surprise when Karen had agreed to a café lunch so quickly – she'd always kick up a fuss when it was suggested in the past and always came up with some line about them serving food in pubs these days so what's the fuss about. It had always been acceptable to the group to order a coffee-based drink while eating in a pub as long as it was ordered with the meal or the order was given to a waiter: as long as nobody had to order it at the bar.

Karen and the other women in the group found it easier to order soft drinks and were often assigned the task.

This time, though, his proposal had met with her immediate approval. Karen without thinking had pointed to the greasy-spoon café they're sitting in now, and had suggested they enter.

As with the last one, Karen knocks back her cappuccino in one hit, tequila slammer style, following it this time with a small belch and a wink.

He supposes that, since his departure from the group, things have changed. That visiting coffee bars is now a regular occurrence, and they have succumbed to the trend of sipping water in pubs – or find it at least acceptable. He supposes this until he remembers a recent conversation with Steven and Jay – when they'd tried to convince him that wine didn't actually count as alcohol.

Once sandwiches and rolls have been consumed, they start to walk the mile back to Adam's flat. She wants to get a taxi, so they stop in at a local cab office and wait. They're told the cab will be about half an hour. Adam feels a little stress at this. He knows it takes fifteen minutes to walk and realises how much he likes walking. How often he does it. He'd probably walked a mile before breakfast around his flat pretending to be Alastair Sim. It's relaxing, walking; what he hates, what he finds unbearable, is waiting.

After waiting forty minutes, they're told the car will be there in only another half hour. By now Karen is beginning to share his hate of waiting, and has developed the additional hates of cabs, cab radio controllers and passengers waiting for cabs (Adam excepted). She suggests they take the bus.

'It can only be about eight stops,' she says.

'No, it's five stops,' he says. He had passed them on the way to the cafe.

They leave the cab office and look for a bus stop. He tells her again that his flat is only fifteen minutes' walk. He points to it; they can just see it from where they're standing. They walk to the nearest bus stop – in the opposite direction to the flat, and wait another twenty minutes. They are now six stops from his flat.

The bus arrives immediately. A few moments after sitting down it happens:

'Tickets please,' says a ticket inspector, appearing from nowhere.

'Eureka!' Adam shouts (he'd meant to say bingo).

Adam concentrates. He composes himself, he thinks about the subtext, then looks at the ticket inspector and says, 'Yes, inspector?'

'I just said. Tickets. Please.'

'Oh.'

He passes his ticket for inspection, chuffed at his performance and wishing Yvette was here to see it. At the next stop he looks out of the window hoping another inspector will get on; suddenly he is starting to like buses. Next time, he decides, he'll be more inquisitive with that phrase; perhaps he'll raise an eyebrow.

Karen hasn't picked up on his Alastair Sim impression. She does, though, ask him why he shouted 'Eureka!' at a bus inspector.

Magnolia

THUD.

Karen examines the wall around his window frame. She does this for a while, from different positions and a range of heights, before pulling the blinds and joining Adam on the sofa.

THUD.

They sit in the comfy sofa, in silence, watching the green fabric draped over the television and listening to the sounds of sock-ball. Adam sips green tea, Karen sips whisky – a remnant of the drinks collection he'd thought about throwing on many an occasion but had saved for guests.

'How's that loser Sockball?' Karen asks.

THUD.

'He's not a loser, he just likes sock-ball.'

She laughs at him. 'You're friends with Sockball.'

THUD. 'Strike one.'

'We're neighbours.'

Karen has been looking at all the walls in the flat since they arrived back from lunch, not just the window area. Eventually, after half a cup of whisky she makes a comment about the decorating:

'They didn't do a good job, did they?'

THUD.

Adam had decorated the flat himself. He always did. Karen, however, somewhat disappointingly had a fondness of decorating parties, especially when she was moving flat.

'They who? I painted that!'

'Ah.' She nods, trying to suppress her own eureka moment.

'It will do,' he says.

'Hmmm. You can still see the underlying colour coming through.'

THUD. 'Strike two.'

This is the toll friends take on your life: irritation. He stops himself from telling her that his life has been busy and he had given decorating as much time as he could – no justification should be required. Besides, it will do!

They sit in silence while she makes a mental note. Another look he has seen before – she'll make a note and talk about it to the first person she can find, adding that she couldn't do a half job like that.

It was once him, the person she'd call, after Jay and before Steven. She'd want them to acknowledge it: that she'd do a better job of decorating; that she's a better person than somebody else; that she takes more care over her appearance; that she is crazier; that she's wilder: that she can not only drink more lager but hold it too.

'Your flat is very well decorated though,' he says, giving her what she wants.

He's surprised at how happy this comment makes her. He'd been patronising, and she hadn't noticed. Why should she? It's not like him to play games.

'It's not that bad,' she says, looking more intensely at his walls. 'I like magnolia and, OK, you can see the paint behind it but ... cream and magnolia aren't too bad a combination.'

'No.' He sips his tea.

Adam retreats to the kitchen under the pretence of making

snacks, and paces around the kitchen table as Alastair Sim. The events of the last few minutes have reminded him of how bad things can get with Karen. The stresses on him are unbearable, and yet he knows that for some reason Karen is trying to hold back; she thinks she is being nice about his neighbour Sockball, nice too about his decorating skills. She is making an effort.

On the second circuit of the kitchen he pulls out some plates and assorted snacks from the cupboards. Then stops abruptly: a noise from the lounge brings him to a halt – the distinctive sound of television set switching on. Cocking his head to one side, taking a single step towards kitchen door, holding his breath, he listens more intently; briefly, he fears for his goldfish, then continues to pace. Recently – since turning it into an Alastair Sim hobby – he has found that though pacing is more enjoyable, it's losing its impact as a way of solving his problems. Inspiration now prefers to turn up while he's buying something, or while queuing for something he intends to buy (minor realisations are more likely to occur while buying garibaldis, for example). He checks the cupboards: there are plenty of biscuits, so there's no excuse to leave the flat.

Something about Karen's arrival is bothering him. Something he suppresses. After Yvette's letter, and its list of negatives, he's trying to eliminate his flaws, one by one. And today's flaw is suspicion.

Returning to the lounge, he switches off the television set and sits back down beside her on the sofa, placing a bowl of salted peanuts and a plate of crispbread between them.

Karen turns towards him, makes direct eye contact, and says something he had not been expecting.

She says, 'I don't want to be friends. That is, I don't

want … just to be friends.'

She tells him she's felt this way for a long time – ever since they met: ever since he'd turned to her as a stranger in the street and accused her of following him.

Adam now feels her warm hand pressed against his thigh. It's been there for a while and yet he's only just noticed. Adam tries to talk himself into it. Sex? Karen looks at him as if she can't make it any simpler to understand.

Really he should have devised a weighting system for those lists. Surely some characteristics are of higher importance than others, especially for friends who might cross the boundary to the realm of lover. Yes, he thinks her attractive. Yes, he always had. No … he couldn't think of a no. Surely there must be a no.

'I thought we could …'

'No,' he says.

'No,' he says again.

'Adam. I know you like me.' She gets closer. Pressing herself against him, her nipples against his chest. He doesn't move away. Crying women are not his only weakness.

She gets closer. He feels the full outline of her breasts pressing against him now. She whispers, 'Steven told me, you wanted me. You want me.'

She hates coffee. She prefers to be in the pub. She insists on it. In the years they've known each other, there has never been a single coffee meeting until today.

When had Steven told her about his feelings for her?

Why him, last night? Two o'clock with tears – it's most unlike her. He'd never seen her cry before. Over a man he'd never met? The least emotional person he'd ever known. A female Don Juan.

Why come to him, and not Jay. Jay is much closer to

her than he, emotionally, physically too – less than half the commute.

'You seen much of Jay lately?'

'I don't hang out with them much these days.'

How strange: it is true, she hadn't been there on the first night, the night he'd been abducted and shown a shallow grave.

She had been at the wedding yesterday, of course, but Adam had been preoccupied with other matters. He can't recall if she'd been there with somebody, or on her own; she wasn't with anybody the last time they saw each other, before his excommunication. So this guy, the guy that's making a strong woman cry, he must be new.

And if she was with somebody yesterday at the wedding, they didn't seem like they'd been arguing: she hadn't shown any sign of distress.

'Name three Alastair Sim films,' he asks, for no reason he can think of.

Counting one with her fingers she says, 'ONE … Don't be ridiculous.'

Why was she trying so hard to be like him? It's not in her nature. Yes, he's a leopard that's changed his spots, but with her it's happened too quickly.

'OK, apart from the St Trinian's movies' – her eyes show a look of recognition – 'name one other.'

'You know I don't care for black and white movies.'

So why does she pretend she does? Coffee bars too.

'So how do you like your sex? Hard and fast, or slow and tantric?'

He had fancied Karen forever, despite her negative qualities. It's not just her ample breasts. She has a real animal quality to her. He is sure they'd be great in bed.

He thinks of bodies pressed tightly together.

156

'Look, I'm a loner. I like being on my own, not part of that group. It's not going to work,' he bleats, fighting the urge to give in.

'You think you're so refined, drinking your coffee from china cups, but you still eat cheesy rolls, don't you!'

A pause, while he looks for her point.

'Shouldn't you be eating canapés. Or …'

He waits for the rest of the sentence, but it doesn't arrive; her face is struggling to come up with an 'or'.

He does like cheese rolls. He does like coffee served in a china cup. He doesn't find the two 'likes' to be mutually exclusive. And, over the last month, has drunk coffee from a variety of containers including the waxy plastic ones in the cinema.

'I like you,' she finally peeps out.

'I like you too. It's just I can't stand being with you. I know it's selfish but – look, I can't remember what I said in the pub when I said goodbye, but they were my reasons.' He will have to practise this. He needs to find a more delicate way of putting it, next time.

'No. I like you … It's a chemical thing.'

At this moment Adam realises that his snacks are being squashed – Karen is sitting on them. This isn't a problem for the peanuts, they're able to deal with the weight of the woman's buttocks, but the crispbread are showing signs of distress and need replacing.

In the kitchen, he again finds refuge: first he eats the damaged crispbread, then replaces them with new ones.

He's not one of those habitual daters. He doesn't need a new lover just because he's stopped seeing an old one (or because she has stopped seeing him). Besides, he's taking a holiday from his love life: six months without one.

He imagines them kissing. He imagines them going

further – isn't that what he's always really wanted?

Quickly now, he starts to pace.

Maybe he should take up serial dating. Yvette obviously thinks he's some kind of nutcase. Is that what nutcases do? he wonders, then dismisses the thought.

After several revolutions of the table he stops. The kitchen table is still covered with torn paper – the lists he's written about his friends and lover, and the letter, all of which he'd ripped into pieces. He sits and looks at them.

He should have kept those lists, all the negatives, as reminders in hours of weakness, in hours of loneliness when he's tempted to pick up the phone and call somebody inappropriate. Or do something inappropriate.

He clears some space on the table; pulls from the table drawer a single sheet of white paper and starts to write. At the top he scribbles her name, 'Karen'; underneath it he writes 'The Lust', scribbles it out and writes 'The List' (he's starting now to believe in the Freudian significance).

Karen and Yvette, they're completely different, that's got to be a positive.

They rarely argued, Adam and Yvette. Maybe they should have. Isn't it supposed to be healthy, a little arguing: venting your anger rather than hiding one's angst? Could this have been their real issue: that they were just too compatible, too similar?

Yvette just wasn't irritating enough. There was very little about her that annoyed him – he looks at the torn lists on the table. Karen, though, is full of irritation: her personality trait deficit was the highest of all his ex-friends, and yet suddenly it's getting harder to remember the negatives. Already he's forgotten about the stresses of the last hour.

People always become more attractive when they fancy you. And yes, there is, as Karen puts it, a 'chemical thing' between them.

Adam stops writing: there's something about the last few minutes that troubles him, something about Karen's declaration.

Spreading out the pile of torn paper on the table, he looks through the fragments, looking for evidence – looking for the last segment of Yvette's letter. He clears a space on the table, then systematically looks through and shifts paper until he finds it: a small torn section of paper which concludes the letter, the letter which had informed him that his services as a lover were no longer required. It reads:

Adam. I don't love you – it's a chemical thing.

Now he thinks of it, the letter shares other characteristics with his ex-friends, there are other similarities: phrases and references that sound like they have much more to do with his ex-friends than his ex-lover. He recollects a paragraph on page seven, for example, which refers to his lack of knowledge of the fashion industry; another paragraph talks about his lack of enthusiasm for all things Australian; another, the fact that he does not like a drink.

Shall he go for a signed confession now? Or shall he elicit some more information?

THUD.

Adam walks calmly into the lounge. Karen is watching television again. He switches it off, gently sits down next to her on his now not-so-comfortable sofa, then places the evidence onto the table in front of her.

THUD.

'Why are you defending him?' she says.

'Who?'

THUD.

'Sockball – the guy is throwing dirty socks at the wall.'

Adam's very sure they're not dirty. Sockball would be appalled by the thought; it's …

'It's against the rules.'

'What?'

'Of sock-ball – you can't throw dirty socks.'

'Rules of sock-ball – see, the guy's a loser.'

Adam loses his patience. If there was a biscuit within reach, he would eat it.

Feeling a strong desire to protect the reputation of his friend Sockball, he asks Karen to leave, and after rearranging his fridge magnets, she does.

A few moments later, in the kitchen, he checks them. They now spell: 'nobody fancies you'; a relief really, given the circumstances.

He spends the rest of the evening in the kitchen, looking out of the window for his bird friend, and looking at the kitchen table, at his letter in bits and pieces.

15

The Cinema Owner

Yvette is back this morning from her long weekend break, so this is the first day of their actual separation – or would be, if he knew for sure whether they were separated or not.

Given his revelations about Karen last night, he is now entertaining the possibility that the letter from Yvette may have been faked, sent by his mafia wannabe ex-friends. Karen too may have been sent round to spy on him, sleep with him. He was about to confront her on this issue when he'd snapped while defending his neighbour's reputation, and had thrown Karen out.ff

Was he really dumped? Is he being too suspicious about his ex-friends? Did they think that getting together with Karen would be a way to entice him back to the group? He has no idea.

Standing at the traffic lights, on the corner of the street next to his office building, he turns and looks towards the patisserie: there's nobody there. He checks his watch – eight fifty-five – and looks again: still nobody: the menu board has not yet been put out, there are no windows being cleaned, there is no Yvette.

The lights change.

Trusting that the traffic has stopped, head still fixed on the patisserie, he crosses the road and continues to walk. Just as his view is obstructed by his office building, he glimpses a woman exiting the patisserie.

Adam stops, takes one step backwards, and observes her writing in chalk on the menu board.

He decides today to use the side entrance and walks towards it, along the street, on the opposite side of the road to the woman.

Within a few steps he knows it's not Yvette, it's one of her waitresses, but continues anyway and walks to the office without glancing again at the café.

Adam keeps to himself for most of the morning; then, at eleven forty-one, he locks the door to a meeting-room and pulls the blinds.

Pace. Mutter. Eyebrows. Sit.

Coincidences occur, yes. But what are the chances of a woman – an ex-friend say, an almost-lover – using in conversation the same phrases Yvette does in her letter?

He remembers the closing statement where Yvette apparently had written, *'I don't like you – it's a chemical thing'*; was this simply coincidence?

And it is not just Karen's words that appear to have been used. Steven too, and Jay and Mark, all had their metaphorical thumbprints on the letter.

Tea is gulped. Biscuits are munched. He checks his watch: eleven forty-two.

The only way to be sure is to ask her. Just come out with it. Has she dumped him? Did she send him that letter? The more he thinks about it, the more it puzzles him. Would Yvette really send him a packet of HobNobs? Plain

HobNobs? If she did send them, why wouldn't they be the dark chocolate kind? For not very much extra money you get a thick layer of dark chocolate on every biscuit.

Gulp. Munch. Eleven forty-three.

Even if she has left him – an occurrence that's looking less likely by the second – there is the programme. There's Screen Seven to save. What choice does he have? The fate of the cinema programme rests on his shoulders now and on an imminent meeting with the Cinema Owner. A meeting, organised a week ago, scheduled prior to receiving the letter, is his only hope of saving the programme, his last opportunity of seeing the kinds of films he lives for – unless he wants to go to London.

Gulp. Munch. Eleven forty-three.

Another look at his watch – a double take: the time is still eleven forty-three? Has time stopped, he wonders? Or is it his watch? He looks again, staring intensely: eleven forty-four.

Gulp. Munch. Eleven forty-four.

The meeting with the Cinema Owner had been arranged for midday. Adam arrives at five past. The Owner arrives at ten past. In the intervening five minutes Adam and Yvette scramble together papers and scribble notes – a flurry of activity with no time for chitter-chatter. Yvette appears stressed on his arrival but kisses him on the cheek – an aggressive peck. She says nothing about any letters, about him being a psychotic madman, about him not listening, about any of his other supposed character flaws.

After they've changed the film title on the top of their canvassing sheets from *Monsoon Wedding* to *Lawless Heart*, and after she has provided Adam with a disapproving glance (he has added a few false signatures to the bottom of the lists – a dishonesty easily spotted), they march into the meeting.

The Cinema Owner has the face of a man who finds life irritating. The rotund, beady-eyed fellow, squelched between a wall and an oversized mahogany desk, peers at their list of signatures, their petition to keep the Screen Seven programme open: two hundred and seventy names claiming they not only want to see it running but are looking forward to seeing what was supposed to be the next film: *Lawless Heart*.

'Why would I keep screening these lousy indie things? Why would these people want to see them?' he says, shaking his head, rising from his seat, about to bring the meeting to a close.

Yvette seizes her chance and launches into her routine. It's a routine that Adam has seen work on a number of occasions while canvassing but to which the Cinema Owner appears impervious. Adam catches her at the appropriate moment.

'They won't come,' says the Cinema Owner.

'The films just need a little local publicity, that's all,' Yvette says, then gives Adam a wide-eyed what-the-heck-do-we-do-now glance.

Adam joins in: 'Don't you see. Now you're closing the programme, people will want to come.'

'What is he prattling on about now?' the Owner asks Yvette.

She replies with a vacant stare and Adam continues, nodding as he speaks: 'Now, you see, the grass is greener. Once the programme is closed people will want to come.'

The Owner looks at him as if this second statement hadn't shed any more light on the matter. Yvette is such a great orator that by comparison Adam feels weak, a let-down; he must put more effort in, expand arguments further, add a bit of charisma, a bit of authority, a bit of Alastair Sim (and a bit of Yvette). 'We've been collecting signatures; look at them,' he says. 'The people on that list, and hundreds more we've told, believe you've cancelled the programme.'

Adam wrinkles his forehead, and lifts his eyebrows attempting an Alastair Sim stare, but doesn't quite pull it off – he's not sure of the subtext. He takes a moment. To the surprise of the Cinema Owner, Adam gets up, paces around the room, mutters something inaudible, opens the door, walks through it, walks a circuit of the cinema foyer, muttering, passing the confectionery counter, the hot dog stand and the coffee machine. Picking up speed, he arcs around the ticket office, faster and faster he walks, pacing and muttering, before returning with confidence, with purpose, back across the foyer, back through the office door, sitting down in his chair, and squaring up to the Owner. He pulls the stare of his life: an immaculate, listen-very-carefully-this-is-important Alastair Sim stare, bulging his eyes and raising his eyebrows, and says:

'It's like when you lend a book to somebody. You lend it because you don't want to read it at that moment. But as soon as it's gone, you miss it. You want to read it again, don't you?' Adam himself only reads a book a second time after it's lent and returned, and trusts the Owner is also the lending kind.

'Supposing you have a book on your shelves at home, about personality types, say – do you possess such a book?' he continues.

'No,' says the Owner.

'Oh, do you have any shelves?'

'No.'

'Oh, do you have in your possession any books at all?'

'No.'

'Well, let us assume you do. And it's on your shelf, and a friend turns up and wants to borrow it. You lend it to the man, an ex-friend for example, because you don't wish to read it at the moment ...' Adam sneaks a little closer to the Owner and lowers his voice. 'But as soon as it's gone, for some reason you realise you liked that book, you need it. The whole notion of there being a limited number of personality types and that we all fit into one of them becomes very interesting. Do you see?'

'Does it?'

'Yes. You find you want to read that book again.'

'Do I?'

'Yes.'

'But I don't like books.'

And he doesn't.

But the Owner does like non-mainstream films, Adam tells him, maybe not so much at the moment, but once upon a time he must have, or else why set up the programme in the first place?

To Adam and Yvette's surprise, the Owner agrees.

'Yes, I liked them,' he says. 'It's just that people aren't interested in seeing these films any more, doesn't matter how much publicity you create. Take the last film, *Monsoon Wedding* – we had a number of people pre-booking tickets for that show. Like you said, the programme was gonna close, people realised what they were gonna miss out on and booked up weeks ago, in advance, so many people that I was thinking about keeping the programme going. But for some reason they all cancelled at the last moment. It's as if somebody was going around, roaming the streets, scaring them off. So, no, I don't believe it, people say they will come, but they won't, I don't care how many signatures you have, I will not resurrect this programme.'

Panicking now, Adam pulls another Alastair Sim stare: Pace. Mutter. Sit. Eyebrows.

It has no effect.

'You're nuts,' the Owner says. 'Lunatics, both of you.'

Adam is wondering whether it would make a difference if he was wearing his Hawaiian shirt, when Yvette joins in.

'WE'LL BLOCK-BOOK THE CINEMA,' she shouts. 'We'll come to an arrangement, buy all the tickets up front!'

'Oh?' says the Owner.

'OH?' Adam repeats, in a slightly less optimistic tone.

Yvette nods. The Owner doesn't think them lunatics now. No. Now they are customers; they're asked if they'd like drinks.

'When did you come up with an idea like that?' Adam asks, after the Owner leaves the room to get them a cappuccino and a latte.

'While you were playing for time.'

'Ah,' he says, pleased he'd been of assistance but hurt she hadn't recognised his impression.

He rocks back in his chair. The door is open and through it he sees the Owner at the coffee-counter putting cups onto tray.

'Don't worry,' Yvette says. 'I have a plan.'

Adam, spying on the Cinema Owner through the gap in the door, is aware that he has been worrying but is surprised to hear it had been obvious to her. He continues to spy on the Owner, watching the fellow, who now is in the confectionary section, by the pick-and-mix. The Owner's big sweaty hand wavers over the flakes. The same hand which had a few seconds earlier been involved in, let's call it, an unpleasant and unhygienic pastime now swoops

167

sideways and down into the chocolate crunch before returning tightly clenched and covered in confectionery. Crunch in hand, the Owner pauses, looks towards his feet, bends over and picks up a plastic cup from the floor, into which he places the crunch.

Adam rocks forward in his chair.

'Don't eat the chocolate crunch,' he tells Yvette, and rocks back again.

Pieces of chocolate now glued to the Owner's hand are picked off one by one and thrown into the cup.

After wiping his hands, the Owner makes his way back to the room.

Adam and Yvette are presented with two white coffees and some chunky chocolate crunch topping in a small dirty plastic cup.

One cup, a white coffee, is placed in front of Adam.

'One cappuccino,' says the Owner.

The second cup, another white coffee, is placed in front of Yvette.

'And one latte.'

Was this the man who devised the coffee machine with the sticky labels? Adam had thought the cinema's coffee fiascos were the result of a faulty dispensing machine, that the labels on the machine were somehow valid and that the machine was at fault in dispensing the same coffee mixture irrespective of which button was pressed. He now has his doubts.

The third cup is placed between the two of them.

'... And some chocolate crunch.'

The Owner, pleased with himself, sits waiting for applause, gratitude at least.

They say nothing.

The Owner jumps back out of his seat, 'Oh, sorry' – he

swaps over the coffee cups – 'all looks the same to me. Coffee is coffee, isn't it?'

'No it's not,' says Adam.

'Thank you,' says Yvette. 'It smells nice.'

It is the most unpleasant-smelling coffee Adam has had in years, but aware of Yvette's desire to make a good impression – something about the way she said thank you – he takes a sip. The coffee in the cinema had always tasted terrible. Usually he masked the flavour with a chocolate flake or chocolate crunch, but doubting the cleanliness of the additives presented to him in the plastic cup, he sips the coffee unadulterated.

Adam takes his time to decide if his drink really is the worst coffee he has had in his life. He takes several more sips and decides if not the worst white coffee in the world, it has to be the worst cappuccino. His cup is almost empty when he realises he has not been paying attention.

Yvette eats congealed chocolate crunch with a spoon, which she licks clean and stuffs into her inside coat pocket.

'Well, that's a deal then,' she says, standing up, grasping the Owner's hand and giving it a good shake. 'Two thousand pounds.'

OK, so he didn't listen this time. This is the first time it has happened while with Yvette, though, and for this he blames his ex-friends: it would not have occurred to him – not listening to Yvette – if they hadn't planted the thought in that letter. A letter which, given their interaction in this meeting, could not have come from Yvette.

'I should warn you' the Owner says, lips pursed, holding back a smile. 'They don't like non-mainstream around here. It makes them restless.' Then, rather dramatically, and with a full blown smirk, he leans across his desk. 'It's something they get angry about.'

The Owner tells them again about the last non-mainstream film in Screen Seven, *Monsoon Wedding*: about how they had to call the police. The box office and confectionery section had been attacked. 'Disgruntled customers,' the Owner says with a certain smugness, 'can prove a nuisance.'

On their way out, Yvette clasps Adam's hand.

'Thanks for the support, you were really great in there,' she whispers as they leave the cinema.

Pushing through the exit swing doors, they're hit with a blast of sunshine. For Adam, it's always a joy leaving the cinema on a bright crisp day. One of the benefits of watching a film in the afternoon is in the blast of light you can get when you leave; the sensation of moving from the dark surround into daylight reality often excites him, fills him with the hope and possibility that the rest of his day might be as interesting as the adventure on screen.

The door swings shut behind them. Standing in the shade, Yvette squeezes his arm. 'All that deep, silent, ponderous thought and head movement,' she says, softly. 'It's very you … And a bit Alastair Sim. You know, you remind me a bit of him. Anybody ever told you?'

'Mannerisms too,' she continues. 'Except for the eyebrows. Alastair Sim rarely moved his eyebrows, or creased his forehead. You know you have very expressive eyebrows?'

'Ah.' He nods.

'What was that film he—'

'*The Green Man.*'

'Yes, *The Green Man.*'

The Deal

While Yvette uses his bathroom, preparing herself for bed, Adam paces his flat as himself, deep in thought. Two thousand pounds to see a film at Screen Seven – it was a bold move, but how much could they possibly hope to recoup?

Pacing, he does three laps of the lounge, (one as Alastair Sim – it slips in without him realising), and looks for the positives.

The other day, in the bookshop, he'd made a conscious decision to stop zoning out in meetings. He'd decided to change, and yet here he is having closed a deal with the Cinema Owner without his knowledge.

Is this what he wants – his subconscious making deals without his consent? Perturbed, he slips into bed, and waits for Yvette.

In the meeting, they had picked a film to screen, or rather one not to cancel. Adam had nodded his approval. They had negotiated a price for block-booking the whole screen; Yvette, knowing this is what Adam does for a living, had left the negotiations to the expert. Adam had been silent; he had appeared disinterested once the Owner was hooked, and had nodded after a lengthy silence to close a deal block-booking the cinema for two thousand pounds.

'Do you think we can recoup the money?' she says, sliding up to him, clean and clingy.

Adam retorts with appropriate and supporting words, while resigning himself to a financial loss.

'Of course, it's our cinema now,' she says. 'Between one thirty and three thirty on Friday – it's ours.'

And so it is. In a way, it's what Adam has always dreamed of: his own private screening room.

16

The Love Birds

Despite a lack of bananas the morning bodes well. It's a sunny day, Adam has woken with Yvette beside him, the cupboards are well stocked after his recent trip to the supermarket, there is plenty for breakfast, and Freddie – the name he's given to the blackbird – has found a mate.

The birds have been singing together, at two o'clock in the morning, in unison, and, yes, both out of tune.

Over breakfast, which consists of warm croissants, jam, biscuits, fruit and coffee – food which is readily available from Adam's kitchen cupboards and eaten quickly before Yvette rushes off to open the patisserie – they discuss their new screen-saving plan and agree to meet later.

After she's gone, Adam peers through the window at the happy feathered couple. You have to presume they're happy, the birds – it's difficult to tell with them: they're always singing, aren't they – singing, for them, is not a sign of being in a good mood.

Something bothers him for the rest of the morning, and at two thirty, after a home-cooked lunch, he decides to be proactive.

He calls the Cinema Owner.

'Hello. I wonder if we may do something about the coffee-making facilities?' he says.

'Who is this?' The Cinema Owner replies.

'Adam. Adam King.'

There had been a real problem with the coffee machine. He is sure the Owner had told him it wasn't working; but fixing it, or getting it fixed when you can't tell the difference between coffee and cappuccino, is not an easy task.

'Ah. Adam. As I said at the meeting. Coffee is coffee, isn't it?'

Adam relaxes his jaw. Unclenching it enough to speak.

'No.'

The Owner laughs. 'Coffee isn't coffee?'

'Certainly, coffee is coffee. And, how can I put it … cappuccino is cappuccino.'

'So a cappuccino isn't a coffee?'

'A type of coffee, certainly. It's like money, our debt to you. We owe you some money, two thousand pounds is money. Two pounds is also money. Do you see my point?'

The Owner gets into a short fluster, and after a little grumbling and some heavy panting, tells Adam, 'I'll make some changes.'

'Thanks,' says Adam.

'Which one's the cappuccino again?' says the Owner.

A few minutes later, after the chat, Adam feels relieved; then it strikes him that it is three o'clock and he is supposed to be at work. With all the excitement – with waking up with Yvette and the news of the blackbirds and the worry about coffee-making facilities – he'd completely forgotten.

The Screen Savers

The patisserie is busy but quiet. The quietness, as usual, punctuated with sounds of slurping and the '*mmms*' and '*ahhs*' of gratification. Occasionally, while waiting for refills or between mouthfuls of cake, small groups start to chatter.

Adam and Yvette have been waiting for ten minutes when Mr Geoff Porter arrives, accompanied by a small familiar figure stroking a cat.

They stand by Adam's chair, both smiling at him.

'I've brought a new volunteer,' Mr Geoff Porter snorts, to Adam's dismay. Yvette recruited Geoff after the last screening, and now the fellow, on his first day, has the temerity to recruit his own volunteer! Where will it end, Adam wonders, staring bleakly into the eyes of his unexpected recruit.

'Geeza!' the Cat Man says to Adam, as though they were best friends, as though he hadn't squealed to the policeman over Adam's little petnapping joke, as if he'd gone to the trouble of actually thanking Adam for his help in searching for that stupid cat, as if they'd known each other forever.

After introductions are made, the new volunteer, stroking Harley, his cat, asks if it's the sort of establishment which might be prejudiced against pets. Yvette tells him it isn't, provided a few pet-handling guidelines are followed, and orders drinks.

'Geeza – what's your fish called?' the Cat Man asks, like

Adam's in the habit of keeping any old kind of fish, like he's in the liberty of keeping a pet trout. It's a ridiculous notion.

'Charlie, and it's a GOLD-fish.'

The Cat Man nods.

'Geeza! Charlie and Harley! My, my.'

It's a speech pattern that Adam feels could prove irritable.

Naturally, the patisserie cappuccino being a new experience for their two new recruits, they talk about the coffee for a full ten minutes. Then, pointing his finger at Adam and Yvette, the Cat Man changes the topic.

'Geeza! Adam and Eve! My, my.'

Adam had always thought pointing in public to be bad manners. The Cat Man, sensing this, lowers the offending digit.

'And would you kindly refrain from calling me Geeza!'

Adam and Eve. He is surprised it has taken this long. It already seems likely that, if his relationship with Yvette were to last, the connection between their names and the biblical characters may – after a couple of hundred references – start to grate; one of them, eventually, would have to change their name.

Yvette shuffles some papers noisily, creating a distraction, then gives the Cat Man their mission statement. She tells him about their successes to date, the signatures they've received and the streets they've covered while canvassing, and she tells him about the upcoming screening of the film *Lawless Heart*.

A second round of cappuccinos arrive, and, based on the look and smell alone, Mr Geoff Porter immediately orders a third.

'It's no longer about merely getting signatures,' Yvette

tells them. 'It's about inspiring them to take that risk and turn up to see this film.'

The Cat Man, stroking his cat, listens to Yvette tell the story of how she had met Adam and why saving the programme is so important: about how it was her parents' favourite cinema and the place of her conception.

She talks about Adam and his fondness for watching films on his own and the sacrifice he is making just in tolerating other people being in the screening room, about how he'd prefer it if he was sitting there in the cinema watching the film completely alone.

'No mobile phone interruptions,' the Cat Man interjects, 'no drunks, no kids, no letting off sounds of any kind, smells of any kind—' then quietly '—and if you happened to let off a smell of any kind, there's nobody else there to smell it: no embarrassing moments.'

Yvette laughs at Cat Man's vulgarity.

Adam shifts in his chair. In his experience, life, quite unexpectedly, can be full of embarrassing moments – it's something you have to get used to.

The Cat Man tells them that he too likes to go to Screen Seven where they show less mainstream films; that he goes there on his own at midday – to the lunchtime screening – when the screening room is empty; that he sits in the middle; that he'd heard about their plan some time ago and that he'd seen their posters while looking for his cat and wants to help.

It has never occurred to Adam to try the midweek, midday screening at Screen Seven. That would obviously interfere with his lunch. This man seems – and Adam is not making a first-impression judgement here, because he's seen the Cat Man at least twice now – rather fanatical for his liking.

'We'd like you to join us but there's an interview to attend – we can't have just anybody saving Screen Seven, I'm sure you understand. We have an image to maintain.'

Quite unexpectedly from Yvette, Adam receives what can only be described as a scowl.

'We'd like it if you could help,' she says, Yvette, smiling like she's genuinely pleased with the assistance.

'Great. So I'm one of The Screen Savers.'

'Good,' says Mr Geoff Porter finishing his fourth cappuccino. 'Welcome to the group. We are The Screen Savers.'

Geoff Porter puts his hand into the middle of the table, and like in a scene from some sort of comic book, clenches his fist.

Another clenched fist lands on the first – the Cat Man's fist.

Then Yvette's fist.

… Three pairs of eyes on Adam, three fists on the table wait for a fourth.

The Big Chill

'There's a depression coming in from the east,' Sockball says, pointing to the Chilean swaying heavily in the breeze.

'A big wind?' Adam asks, looking at the tree.

'Yes – the biggest for a while.'

A pang of concern – Adam munches a bourbon cream (his experience has taught him that Sockball is not the kind of host who supplies actual biscuits, so this time he'd brought a packet with him).

Together they sip their strong tea while looking at the tree.

Planes are grounded aren't they, in severe winds, but what about blackbirds? Do they fly? Are they aware of the hazards? Adam dunks another biscuit and assumes they must be.

He can't hear them, or see them, the blackbirds, but he is sure they're there, in the tree, sleeping.

The tree is swaying wildly, over-exaggerating the bluster, as if it's seeking attention.

'It's getting colder too,' says Sockball. 'We'll have to start wearing bigger coats soon! Thicker socks too.'

Adam is aware of the changes in temperature – he's worn his big heavy coat now on a number of occasions, and has to make changes to his Alastair Sim, personality-wise, as a result. The coat, which contains a number of strawberry-red horizontal lines and a large quantity of padding, appears to make him look larger than normal, and more jovial. An asset in the mornings when the atmosphere in the hallway is positive or when he's buying his bananas from the fruit shop, but a problem in the evenings when the mood turns darker and a more sinister costume is required.

Wet Feet

The next evening, with their two new recruits, Adam and Yvette canvass.

For the first two streets they work as a team, the Cat Man and Mr Geoff Porter watching Yvette's performance at first, assisting with some of Adam's supporting functions later.

Periodically Yvette's pitch is disturbed as the Cat Man fidgets or scratches, or says something derogatory to prospective cinemagoers he deems unworthy.

After Yvette's insistence that this fellow join their crusade, Adam resists the temptation to put the man in his place.

'Suppose we do something more radical,' says the Cat Man, at the end of the street.

'Like what?' says Yvette.

The Cat Man raises his voice: 'I don't know, these people just need shaking up a little. WE NEED TO BE MORE AGGRESSIVE HERE.' Then whispers: 'They just need a little coercion.'

'Like what?' Yvette says again.

'Blackmail. Petnapping. Whatever it takes. I have a friend who'll get us some guns.'

Could this just be Adam's destiny? They say you meet the same personality types all your life, that you leave one person only to replace them with a copy. He bought a book on the subject once, by mistake – don't ask – which claimed there were only thirteen personality types and that all of us broadly fitted into one category. He cannot recall one of those types being titled *Thinking You're in The Mafia*. He thinks it unlikely. And since the book had been borrowed by one of his ex-friends, checking will prove cumbersome.

Will all his acquaintances have this mafia boss complex?

'There'll be no kidnappings,' he says.

'But you took Harley.'

Adam continues, 'There'll be no rough stuff, just gentle persuasion and a little lying, but that's it.'

Yvette provides a supporting nod.

By the end of the evening they've agreed to separate into two groups, have marked areas on a map for each group to canvass, and have agreed a meeting for a progress report.

———

A few hours later, from the comfort of his own kitchen he checks up on his feathered friend. Peering through the window at the trees, he looks for the two blackbirds: he sees nothing.

SLAP.

The magnets on the fridge still read 'nobody fancies you', but that clearly isn't the case.

SLAP.

Karen is mistaken. Somebody does – as it's so eloquently put – fancy him, and somebody he likes—

SLAP.

'Ouch.'

'Sorry.'

—somebody who at this very moment is slapping his bottom.

SLAP.

Until very recently Adam used to be a cringer – a rare breed of man who dislikes the boy-gets-girl film ending. Boy gets the girl and then what? The end. No more conflict, no more intrigue, the rest of their story is too boring to show you.

Part of Adam is appalled by this, part of him has been determined not to live happily ever after for some time; but with Yvette now he's starting to feel very ... Hollywood.

'It's nice you're jealous.'

'Me? Jealous? Of who?' He continues to look through his binoculars, waiting for a reply. Yvette does not reply – she stops her bottom-slapping game and starts mopping the kitchen floor, starting with his feet.

The Cat Man is a kindred spirit of sorts, he supposes. Clearly they have things in common. And clearly they need help if they're to save the programme.

Another screening like the last one – only eight turning up, and two of them wrecking the foyer in protest – and all will be lost. Either they take the help ... or he will have to go to London.

Besides, there are other more worrying concerns: Adam can't help but feel some liking for their group. This, he fears, is what happens when you're on a crusade: you bond as a team. He will have to watch carefully to make sure things do not get out of hand.

Once the kitchen floor is clean enough and Adam's feet are wet enough, Yvette takes the binoculars from his hand and leads him to the bedroom. A few seconds later, they lie semi-naked on the bed. She clenches her hand and brings it down on top of his chest.

'Go on,' she says, nodding at her fist.

Adam huffs and places his fist on top.

17

The Suppliers

En route to work, he stops at the grocery shop to buy a single banana. Quite why he keeps doing this, he's not sure. It has, well, just become a routine. If he bought three or four bananas he could stock up at home and save two minutes' journey time most days; but there'd be no need to stop there every day.

He likes the smell and the colours, that's it, the atmosphere. It feels like he's in a comedy film set or a musical. It jollies things up a bit. Even if it's cloudy or if he thinks he's been dumped by his girlfriend, or he's moody for any other reason, the 'Fruit Shop', as it's called, is an emotional reset button.

Adam's not the only person to buy a single piece of fruit in the shop. Others do too – there's quite a brisk trade in single fruit buying. So although there's a queue, it moves too quickly for idle chatter and within a few moments, banana in hand, he continues on his morning journey.

Adam hasn't been speaking to the suppliers. But they have

been calling him. He's been too busy, what with eating breakfasts at the patisserie and time off canvassing, to check his voicemail or read faxes, and had learnt a long time ago that he need only work when absolutely necessary.

He hasn't been doing any work, and is pleased to think the company is doing very well without him. His desk certainly has become more tidy since he started to concentrate on saving Screen Seven.

Arriving at it this morning, Adam finds his desk is supporting a number of reports. They've been on the desk for a while, loafing around his in-tray, and somebody, he suspects The Boss, has moved them to a more prominent position – in the middle. He'd planned on reading them two weeks ago, and their change of location indicates the matter may have become somewhat urgent.

Reading them, he sees the reason for The Boss's agitation: they forecast that the company will run out of parts in three weeks – and that was two weeks ago.

He calls the suppliers – their main deal-closer is on holiday until Monday. He'll have to deal with it then, in the morning.

After making a note in his diary and returning the reports to their usual position – the in-tray – he gets on with the business of photocopying.

Busying himself for the rest of the day, he builds up a good mood which lasts until three-thirty, when, leaving the office and heading towards the lifts, he's approached by a woman.

'You going to the office outing?' she asks, clapping her hands together and ever so slightly bouncing up and down on the spot.

The woman before him is nice enough: she reminds

185

him of a potential cinemagoer he'd met out canvassing the previous night. Their conversation at the door had been quite pleasant – she had laughed in all the right places and cheered for an encore after Yvette's closing scene. The half-hour they spent together had been an enjoyable experience; at one point she'd even held his umbrella.

In the corridor, he deliberates in front of the incredible bouncing woman: at the last office outing – last Christmas – they had seen *Oliver!,* the musical, and there had been audience participation. Adam and the whole of the front row were forced to join in; they had to stand up, face the audience, and sing, '*Consider yourself one of the family …*'.

'I think it's unlikely I'll be attending the Christmas event this year, but thank you.'

'You sure? You are invited. All permanents are invited.'

'Yes, I know.'

As they are now engaged in conversation, the woman assumes, as is customary here, that he would like to talk about television.

'You see *EastEnders* last night?'

Adam tells her he did not watch that programme; that he does not watch television. This induces in the woman a silence long enough for him to leave the building.

After work, in the café, the dominant noise is the slurp – a soothing, relaxing kind of slurp backed by the usual *mmms* and *ahhhs* of contentment and accompanied by a short low grumbling grunt, supplied courtesy of Geoff. An uncouth grunt, but mingling with the other café noises it fits in surprisingly well, complementing the atmosphere.

Next to Geoff, The Cat Man sits, stroking Harley his fluffy white cat. Today he's wearing a light linen suit, and for some reason has shaved his head.

'I'd like to declare the third meeting of The Screen Savers open.' Geoff, standing now, is reading from what appears to be a typed sheet.

This bothers Adam a great deal: Geoff is acting like they're running some big corporation when clearly they're just four people drinking lucky dip cappuccino; the man also has with him a clipboard, and is reading from it, a speech he has obviously been practising.

Adam waits for the second sentence before voicing his objections.

Geoff leafs forward and backwards through a wodge of paper clamped to the clipboard.

'I don't think we need get this formal,' Yvette says.

'Oh, right,' Geoff says, and sits.

Noticing the lucky dip cappuccino, Geoff becomes distracted: blowing lightly on the top froth, he uncovers blackberries.

Noticing the wad of paper, Yvette says, 'But as you've gone to a lot of trouble, could you tell us what you think about our canvassing expeditions?'

'Mmmm, well, that is the first point on the Agenda. Point number one,' Geoff says, standing, 'Cat Man thinks we should change the canvassing forms.'

The Cat Man, who has been fishing pomegranate out of his cappuccino since the meeting began, puts his spoon down and tells them that it's not about formatting the form but the whole concept of a petition that's too wishy-washy. They need something more secure.

'We need more than a pledge – an affidavit,' he says.

A group silence.

'That's ... a great idea,' Yvette says. 'What does it mean?'

'It means,' says Adam, 'that we'll need a lawyer to look

at it – any forms – and to witness the signings.'

'I am a lawyer,' the Cat Man announces.

The three of them look at the Cat Man, all of them struggling to believe him.

'Anything else?' Yvette looks again towards the big clipboard.

'Oh, err,' Geoff stands again. 'Point two – the Cat Man think—'

'What we need,' says the Cat Man, cutting in, 'is just one big mainstream audience to watch it. Those cinemas in London. Must have five hundred people there, for an action film. If they were to watch this …'

Doesn't anybody pay Adam any attention? 'London already shows non-mainstream films,' he explains. 'They have whole cinemas dedicated to them.'

'But not enough. There could be more,' the Cat Man says, persisting with his cause of scaling up their efforts. 'For the benefit of society, we must get all cinemas to show this kind of stuff. It is our duty.'

'Anything else?' Yvette, sensing the tension, halts the conversation and looks again towards the big clipboard sitting on Geoff's lap.

'No. That's it.'

Adam and Yvette agree that their new team members are entitled to develop as much awareness as they like in London, but will have to stay focused for now on saving Screen Seven if they want to be part of their … their gang?

Cinema Owner II

At home, Adam makes a phone call. The call is picked up after one ring.

'Would it be—' He's interrupted, by a groan from the Cinema Owner. 'Would it be possible not to dim the lights in our screening room: to switch them off in one hit?'

'No.'

'It's our screening room, Screen Seven, at least for one performance, and we would like them to be turned off in a single hit.'

'You don't own anything: it's my cinema. I am the Cinema Owner,' says the Cinema Owner, with logic seemingly on his side. 'You don't own anything. And we can't change the lighting: it's on a dimmer switch. Automatic.'

And with that the man hangs up.

In a fit of rage, Adam buys a newspaper and paces the flat reading it as Alastair Sim. By the time he has calmed down, he is reading the supplement on fashion. Purple apparently is in fashion.

18

Slap Bang Wallop

'Ouch.'

She slaps her hand against his naked buttocks, lifts their firm flesh a few centimetres, and lets them drop.

'Very pert,' she says, 'and firm, but with just the right amount of give.'

Adam is in his bedroom looking for signs of bird life in the Chilean.

She does it again, faster this time: slapping, raising, dropping, watching.

'Please, I'm busy!' he says, peering through binoculars.

Just using her fingertips she flicks his buttocks, opening and closing her hands one at a time, forcing them up and down alternately.

Then she stops.

He flinches: her teeth bite into his left cheek.

'You ever do this yourself?' she says.

Another bite – the right cheek.

'Ever looked in the mirror while playing yo-yo with your buttocks? I would, if I were you. I'd be playing yo-yo buttocks all day.'

She continues with her game, adding a new comic noise. 'BOING, BOING, BOING, BOING, BOING.'

'Look, you can play with them as long as you stop making stupid noises.'

It goes quiet.

He turns to her and apologises: it's a game Yvette is fond of but Adam abhors – a difference he'd forgotten about during their almost separation.

A difference he likes.

'Why don't you just go out with your real friends, instead of spending your time talking to your blackbird and your goldfish?' she says finally, half an hour later, at bedtime. She slips between the sheets, sidling up next to him. 'They can't be that bad and you're running out of things to do. You can't keep on canvassing forever; what you going to do with your spare time when we stop?'

The Experiment

He struggled while they were away, Sockball and Yvette – he missed them. Also, while out canvassing, on a number of occasions, he has talked with people who seemed less irritating than normal. Is it possible, therefore, that he has made a mistake in giving up on the notion of friendship too quickly?

His grievance may not be to do with the concept of having a friend, but the type of friends he's attracting. Out there, there may well be people he can tolerate, a different personality type to the one he attracts normally; it could just be a question of finding them.

Yes, there are new people in his life – the new Screen Savers – but they're too similar to the old ones, and Frankenstein friends, as he's discovered, just don't exist.

He's got Yvette and Sockball, a lover and a neighbour in his life, but there needs to be more. He needs a new type of friend. A spare he can call on when everybody else is away. A different kind of friend: one who'd break this cycle he's in of reconnecting with the same personality types.

There are all sorts of people out there. Animals too. If a tone-deaf blackbird can find a mate who doesn't mind its chirp, he can find a friend who doesn't think he's in the mafia. He just needs to experiment.

In the fruit shop, queuing for his regular morning banana he decides to test out his theory.

He approaches the Fruit Man as normal. His regular morning banana, already deposited in its brown paper bag, is placed in front of him.

'Hello. I'm Adam,' says Adam, testing the waters of friendship.

Adam holds out a hand and waits. The Fruit Man slaps it, like in some American teen movie.

'Geeza! I am the Fruit King.'

Oh dear. He's just like the Cat Man, who is like Steven. OK, Steven doesn't say 'Geeza' all the time – a positive attribute he'd taken for granted with those ex-friends but …

'You don't happen to like gangster films do you?'

'You talking to me?'

Adam pays for his banana and leaves the Fruit King to his Robert De Niro impersonation. Martin Scorsese has a lot to answer for. Everything except *After Hours* – a less commercial film he'd seen in Screen Seven a number of years ago.

By the time he leaves the shop, he's already peeling his banana. You'd think a man owning a comedy-set fruit shop would be more jovial, more upbeat. And to be fair, he may well be. But a first impression that reminds him of his gangster wannabe ex-friends will not be tolerated. The point of his experiment is to meet a new kind of person.

The problem is his subconscious: it's drawing him to the wrong type of person. If he's going to make a new friend, far better if he has little to do with it, far better that it occurs at random: he'll let fate decide.

Continuing his experiment in the park, sitting on the nearest available bench he closes his eyes (if he can't see a potential new friend, neither can his subconscious), and he waits.

He waits sitting on the bench for some twenty minutes.

Nobody sits next to him – he looks around the park –

why would they? There are plenty of other benches to sit on. The park, apart from him, is still empty.

The accumulation of friends is not as easy as it seems.

He could just fraternise with his work colleagues – there is after all this Christmas outing to go to; or he could just stand in the lobby, saying hello to people as they get into and out of the lift. But he needs a safety valve. If things go wrong, he needs an escape route, and finding a new fruit shop is easier than finding a new job.

Adam tries the bus stop.

Half an hour later somebody joins him: a woman; something he had not anticipated. He sticks to his rules and is about to use a common opening line when he notices it – a large bag of crisps – and decides to hold off on his little friend-making experiment and observe.

She starts to munch, eating crisps one by one: sticking her tongue out quite some distance, placing on top of it a single crisp and retracting, lizard style.

Does he want a lizard friend? How would Yvette feel about his friendship with a new woman? Questions he has difficulty pondering, given the noise that's being made.

You could assume that by using this method of consuming food, the woman would render a noisy snack harmless – that the moisture on the tongue would dampen the crunching sound. It does not. Somehow the noise level increases.

Sensing, maybe, that Adam is disturbed by this, she tries to chomp more quietly.

It's not the poor woman's fault of course. You'd think by now they'd have invented a quiet crisp, wouldn't you? A crisp with a silent crunch. (If they can invent potpourri that smells like biscuits, there should be a crisp with a silent crunch.)

And isn't she entitled to eat a packet of crisps or two in an open air? It's not as if she's in the cinema, is it – this new person he's about to introduce himself to. It's not a negative anyway. Not at the moment.

If a woman wants to eat loud crisps, why shouldn't she?

Feeling pleased with himself – with his tolerant nature – he watches on as the crisps are finished, the packet flattened and folded and stuffed it into a brown leather handbag, from which something else is pulled out – a magazine: a television guide.

Would they get along, this woman and him? What would they talk about, Adam and this new friend of his? He'll not draw any conclusions as to their suitability yet – first impressions are often misleading.

A second woman joins them, sits on the other side of the crisp woman and immediately launches into conversation:

'Did you watch *Frasier* last night?' she says immediately.

The situation is rapidly becoming interesting. And nerve racking. How would he really feel about a normal friend: one who watches television? How would he feel being friendly to, say, a woman who doesn't want to be anybody else – who doesn't want to be in the mafia, doesn't want to be Robert De Niro, or Alastair Sim? A woman who probably thinks tree watching is a ridiculous hobby; staring at green fabric too.

Often it is the case that once you get what you want you realise it's not what you want: it's something you never wanted. Could this be such an occasion?

Turning to make conversation, he sees her getting on a bus, alone, leaving her fellow television-watching friend behind.

He follows her.

The bus is busy, but seats are still available, and he sits behind her, intent on making a few more observations before progressing.

For a couple of stops there is very little to observe: her crisps are eaten; she talks to nobody; she sits in silence, glancing occasionally through the window to her left.

She gets off the bus, he follows. It's a busy street, and she moves quickly. He has to stay close to keep up.

This, at least, is safe. A friend made in these circumstances – randomly and without connection – may be disposed of with ease. If, after they have become friends, he decides a mistake has been made, he can be blunt about the matter – like last time, when he said goodbye to the old group. But this time he could part company with ease.

'Why are you following me?' The woman has turned, and is now looking directly at him.

'Me? Following you? Well, well.'

'Well?'

Well, to be honest, he hadn't thought about this sequence of events from the other side, from her point of view. And now he finds himself in an awkward situation.

'Well, yes, I suppose I was following you. You see …' And then, in simple, plain language he tells her about his situation and his experiment; and noticing her body language, he concludes his speech by saying: 'I'm not a lunatic.'

'People often stop me in the street,' the woman says. 'They confuse me for a celebrity.'

'Oh?' Adam remarks, with intrigue.

The woman, whose name has yet to be revealed, does remind him of somebody. She has a similar personality to Yvette.

'Yes,' the woman says, glowing with pride, 'people think

196

I look like Audrey Hepburn.'

'Audrey Hepburn?'

Adam feels the start of a chicken impression (an expression he is used to seeing rather than performing, facial movements that preempt a look: a kind of she's-not-as-attractive-as-Audrey-Hepburn look). Aware of the impression, and the look – that it may hurt her feelings – he is able to stop himself.

'Yes, but I tell them Audrey Hepburn is dead,' she says.

Adam struggles for a response.

She gives him a look of recognition. 'You look like somebody too.'

'Really?' he says, preparing himself, trying not to preempt a possible positive affirmation with a negative.

'Yes, Clive Owen. Only not so good-looking.'

He's not sure in what way, but she is similar to Yvette. Not in all respects: they have important differences, not just in the TV-watching and crisp-eating departments; but in some respects (and he's not sure what) they are similar, their personality types overlap.

As a friend this woman shows promise, but the problem, the issue, is that because she reminds him of Yvette there could therefore be sexual tension arising between them at some point in the future. And the point is, the point of the experiment is, to find a friend, not a lover – he already has one of those.

He makes an apology and tells her this: about Yvette and personality types and sexual chemistry, and then leaves.

The woman takes the news surprisingly well.

19

Close Encounters of the Friendship Kind

How fickle friendship can be: this morning the Fruit King not only cannot remember Adam's name, but can't even be bothered to make one up like last time (he'd been called 'kid' yesterday, in what Adam likes to think of as 90s American gangster film slang). Today the fellow doesn't even say hello. The Fruit King just gives Adam his banana and says, 'Twenty pence.' Oh, there is a little pause before taking Adam's money, a little glimmer of recognition on the fellow's face, a look that says, *I've seen this man before but can't remember where.*

It's very encouraging. Adam lets it happen without jogging the Fruit King's memory and trundles off to work, contented, happy, pleased the status quo has been re-established.

He's taken so much time off lately that he finds it hard to believe he's got a job. Apart from the call he made the other day to get some spare parts – a report on his desk had forecast that the company is about to run out of parts and he is responsible for buying supplies, so felt duty-bound to make that call – work has become merely a stopping-off point on his way to socialising with Yvette and a starting point for his canvassing campaign.

Today, though, there is cause for concern: scribbled on a pink sheet of paper are the words *'see me'*.

It is ominous – The Boss normally just shouts at him as he passes by his door in the morning; he's never had a formal invitation before, and is aware that The Boss has a tendency to be school-teachery when he's about to fire somebody.

Also, Adam's diary is open – somebody has been looking through it. It's open at this coming Friday – the day of the *Lawless Heart* screening – where he had booked the afternoon off as *'Meeting with Supplier'*.

Waiting in The Boss's office, Adam thinks about time, about how he's barely managing to fill it without television or friends, about how if he's inventive with his new hobbies, he can cope. But without a job? The process of getting to and from work takes an hour alone, and with the Screen Saving under control, occupying himself could be a struggle.

He is seriously considering taking up reading as a hobby when The Boss walks in, talking as he walks:

'Look, I know you've been working hard on these negotiations over supplies. You must have more knowledge on pricing than anybody else in the world by now. I like that, and I won't forget it come bonus day.'

'Thanks,' says Adam.

'Now, you keep on at them, grind them down. They're not going to screw us. You know what they're like.'

'Well, yes.'

The meeting is going far better than expected. Adam

sighs with relief.

'Tell you what,' The Boss continues. 'I'll come along to this meeting on Friday – I'll be quiet, let you do your thing. I'll just be there for extra menace, keep the f*ckers on edge.'

'Oh, I don't think that's necessary,' Adam says, assured that he won't need any help in the meeting, because there is no meeting.

'OK. You let me know, though, if you need some weight in there. You understand?'

Adam nods.

The deal with the suppliers will take a twenty-minute phone call when the supplier returns from his holiday on Monday. No meeting is required, and yet Adam is worried: The Boss doesn't normally give up this easily – without a large bout of swearing and a lot of fluster – and after this much work trying to save Screen Seven he doesn't want to miss Friday's screening because of a fictional meeting.

On leaving The Boss, Adam ventures to the office canteen for lunch where he finds himself queuing next to a man from accounts; a man who knows his name.

Minding his own business, observing the effect of standing in slow-moving lines on his central nervous system, he is faced with the inevitable:

'What you watch on television last night?' A sucker punch. No introductions. No hellos. The man gets straight to the point.

'Nothing,' Adam says, shaking his head.

'What's that? A new game show is it?'

'No, I didn't watch anything.'

'Nothing?'

'That's right.'

They edge along the line in the canteen.

'Out late were you, at some party?'

'No. I stayed at home.'

They each pick up a plate of potatoes and a lamb casserole.

'I've got a portable you can borrow … If you're a bit stuck for a television. What, your tube gone, has it?'

The man plays with his loose sachets of salt, squeezing them like some stress-relieving toy, the tension rising as they inch toward the section marked desserts.

'No. Actually …' For some reason he can't quite figure out, Adam needs a deep breath before finishing his sentence. '… I've given up television.'

'Really?'

'Yes, really.'

He hears the words 'miserable' and 'bastard' muttered as the man leaves the queue without dessert. It's another recurring pattern in his life he'll have to do something about.

Columbo

THUD.

Avoiding television is simple. Assuming that is, that Sockball isn't watching a science and nature programme (which is most of the time). He almost forgets he has one. With the green fabric hanging over the set, it's almost become what-do-you-call-it, camouflaged. So used to seeing it is he that he's starting to forget that it covers anything at all.

THUD.

And supervised access to Sockball's television is also helping. Oh, he has to watch whatever Sockball is watching, and their tastes are not similar, but he's hardly watched his own television now for four weeks.

THUD.

Avoiding television is not as hard as avoiding talking about television; it's the first thing people talk about at work. 'Did you see *EastEnders* last night?' they ask. No, he did not. He saw green fabric, he watched green trees, he listened to chirping. Things people are just not interested in discussing.

THUD.

Right now he is watching sock-ball.

It's becoming a common occurrence for him to be approached about television. In fact, he has become somewhat of a fascination in his office. Something has to be done, he thinks. The next morning, in the fruit shop, a solution presents itself.

Queuing for a banana, he overhears a conversation:

'You watch *EastEnders* last night?'

'Yes, it was good, wasn't it?'

'Yes. You see it, *EastEnders*, then?'

'Yes, it was good.'

He listens to them talking about *EastEnders* for a couple of minutes: thirteen times they mention that it was 'good'. Once they refer to it as 'marvellous' – a comment they do not expand upon.

Then it strikes him. Maybe that's what's happening. Maybe it's all made up. Nobody's watching television. They're just pretending. They don't need to watch it – they just need to talk about watching it. Anything.

Could it be that, just like him, the world has just decided to stop watching television?

At work, queuing for the photocopier, he's given an opportunity to test his theory:

'You watch anything on TV last night?' a robotic voice says, from accounts.

'Yes, I saw *Columbo* last night, good wasn't it?'

The robot from accounts blinks twice.

'*Columbo* wasn't on last night.'

OK, it appears that people do actually watch television all the time. He tries to cover up:

'Yes it was, it was on Sky.'

The man, in a fluster, leaves his file on the desk by the photocopier and walks off.

Adam has almost finished duplicating his flyers when the man returns with a copy of yesterday's television listings.

'I've got Sky and I didn't know it was on,' the man says. 'Show me.'

Adam looks through the television listings. *Columbo* he

thought was always on one channel or another, and he'd distinctly thought he'd heard it last night through the floorboards of his flat. Unless, of course:

'Oh, no, no, no,' Adam says, packing his photocopies in a folder he'd bought specially. 'I saw it on video.'

He walks off down the corridor pursued by the accountant.

'Can I borrow it? The video?'

'We'll see,' Adam says. 'It's a very popular video, a lot of people want to borrow it.' It's a fictional video he'll be pretending to watch a lot from now on.

By the time he's finished his morning banana, there have been seven requests to loan his *Columbo* video. He has to make a list.

20

The Mother

They walk along the streets posting flyers and telling people that there will be a screening of the film *Lawless Heart* on Friday at two p.m. in Screen Seven, and that there will be a free lucky dip cappuccino at the patisserie for anybody producing a ticket stub.

Yvette provides her usual dynamic display, earning them four more signatures within their first half hour on the road. The next door, the door to number twenty-six, opens as they're about to knock.

'Would you like some tea? I've got some garibaldi biscuits,' says a woman in her late fifties.

'Yes, we would,' replies Yvette.

She walks in. Adam follows.

They sit on a not-so-comfortable sofa while the lady makes the tea. Yvette nudges him and nods at a mound of photographs on the table to his right.

The woman brings tea in immediately and places it on the table, nudging the photographs ominously towards them with the tray. She sits in the armchair to the right of the table, keeping them within an easy tea-passing circumference (also within easy photograph-passing circumference). The tea is in a pot. The garibaldis are on the plate, laid neatly, lengthways, their ends touching, forming a circle. Twelve biscuits in total: ten in the circle and two lying idle to the side.

Adam is suspicious of the tea, of water that could boil so quickly.

'I saw the two of you walking down the street, with your papers,' says the woman. 'So I put the kettle on while you were at number twenty-four.'

His suspicion passes.

He is drawn to a large photograph hanging on the wall. It is of a young Steven Hargreaves, one of his abductors, from whom his friendship has recently been excommunicated (birthdays excepted); it shows him at graduation about twelve years ago.

'Mrs Hargreaves?' Adam says.

He stops himself from saying 'you don't live here'; he has learnt not to be so dismissive after his your-name-isn't-Yvette conversation, especially when it's obvious the woman does live here. It's another change he'd notice in himself, another spot knocked off the leopard.

'Yes, Adam?'

He scans the framed pictures on the mantelpiece looking for a group photograph, wondering whether he'd be in it.

'When did you move?'

He considers pouring the tea. It's been fermenting now for too long and he's been given no indication that the tea-distribution is about to commence. Over-brewing is a common tea hazard.

She tells him she moved to the house ten years ago,

about a year after they had last seen each other – Adam had met her a few times while visiting his ex-friend on their university summer breaks.

'Are you aware that your son is a violent criminal?' Adam asks.

'Yes, dear,' says Mrs Hargreaves. 'We talk about everything; share all our worries and concerns – I've got the photographs here.'

Mrs Hargreaves picks up the set of prints, opens the envelope flap, and flicks through photos. Then she stops and pulls one out.

'Here it is, dear.' She passes it to him.

It's of the wedding: of an abducted Adam tied with bandages, Egyptian mummy-like, and with his mouth gagged.

'I wasn't invited—' she chomps a garibaldi – 'what with only being the best man's mother.' She finishes the garibaldi and picks up the remaining one not participating in the two-circle formation.

'And there they go, inviting somebody who doesn't want to be there.' She chomps the biscuit. Another garibaldi gone.

Yvette's hand is on Adam's knee again; it has been for a while. He likes it. Likes not noticing it too, and the familiarity that this implies. It strikes him that Yvette has been quiet throughout the conversation so far – it's most unlike her.

The phone rings.

He half expects it to be her, Yvette, calling him at the house of a kidnapper's mother; and though he's aware that it's impossible because she's sitting by his side, he's half disappointed when it's not.

No, Steven is calling, Steven the son, Steven the

kidnapper, the ex-friend, the leader of the mafia clan.

Mrs Hargreaves excuses herself and makes conversation loudly with her son on the phone: 'Yes, well, they say turquoise is going to be very fashionable next year, dear, though I have a liking for lavender.'

She continues: 'Well, I would, dear, but I can't talk now, I've got guests ... Yes ... They're Jehovah's Witnesses. We're having tea.

'Of course – I wouldn't normally, but one of them is your friend, dear. Adam ... Yes, that Adam, who went to your friend's wedding in fancy dress.'

A long pause.

Adam thinks about Jehovah's Witnesses and tea. Yvette sits quietly in contemplation. Mrs Hargreaves waits for her son to say something.

Mrs Hargreaves continues: 'Yes, the Egyptian mummy ... Yes, peculiar that – for a Jehovah's Witness – isn't it ...' While listening to her son, a look of anguish spreads across her face. She looks up at Adam. 'OK, I'll call you when they're gone. Love you too, son. Bye, bye.'

She wants him to leave.

She puts the receiver down and, very apologetically, asks them both to leave. They don't get to drink tea, or eat garibaldi. They get to be ushered onto the street like unwanted callers invited in by mistake.

They walk down the street in silence, neither of them wanting to make any more house calls today. He thinks Yvette probably guessed part of what went on at number twenty-six, understood part of the conversation they'd caught on the phone. The whole story will have to wait.

At a pelican crossing, waiting for traffic to pass, he hears crunching. Yvette, smiling, is eating a garibaldi.

'Want one?' she says offering him a biscuit.

He takes the biscuit.
'I took two,' she continues.
Later she'll admit to having taken three.

21

The Big Push

After cooking them both a good dinner – a corned beef omelette – Adam stares out of his kitchen window for a while until he notices, once again, that he has wet feet.

Yvette, who this time cleans only the area in which he stands, seems annoyed again by his bird-watching activity and in bed later on refuses to discuss the matter.

'The Cat Man was right,' she says the next morning. 'We do need to do something extra.'

'Yes,' Adam says, presuming this conversation is linked to this shoe-washing habit she has acquired, and looking for a connection.

'The last screening was an evening performance and only a handful of people turned up. It's going to be worse this time,' she says, turning away from him. 'We're running out of time. We need an extra push, just to be sure, in case people don't turn up like last time. We must convene a meeting.'

'A meeting with who?' he asks. 'The Cinema Owner?'

'The group, silly. The Screen Savers. All of us.'

———

In the café, Yvette provides refreshments to their troops –
The Cat Man and Geoff Porter – then calls them to order.

'We need an extra push,' she tells them, 'just to be sure,
just in case people don't turn up – like last time.'

The Cat Man delicately clears away the topping from his
cappuccino then pats his foam lightly with the underside
of his spoon. His lacklustre attitude riles Yvette.

'WELL?' she says, standing, lightly clenching her fists.
Aggression on this level is an emotion Adam's only recently noticed in Yvette, and he likes it.

Yvette sits.

'Come up with a solution and I'll give you free cappuccinos – for life!'

'We could get the students to come, from college – they
could do with a break from watching TV,' Geoff spurts,
panicking.

'Students?' says the Cat Man, with an air of disapproval
that Adam finds comforting.

'Yes. It's a good idea,' says Yvette. 'We need all the people we can get.'

Geoff orders another cappuccino.

'OK,' Adam joins in, 'but only if they're studying quiet
subjects. Like Economics. Or Librarianism. No arts subjects.'

'How about politics?'

The Cat Man and Adam look at each other: Politics students – are they likely to turn up drunk and rowdy? Do
they have a tendency to eat noisy snacks? Are they likely to
talk during the trailers? Or during the main—

'Anybody!' Yvette bleats. 'I already said – we need all
the people we can get!'

The Cat Man makes phone calls while Geoff starts

planning. On a napkin he writes the words 'more recruits', followed by a list of course subjects. A few moments later he stops, grits his teeth, stares intently at the napkin, looks Adam square between the eyes and says: 'We'll need some flyers. Have we got any?'

Yvette, bubbling with energy now, takes Geoff's hand and leads him to a special storeroom: a part of the café which they've devoted to the campaign. Stacked floor to ceiling, Adam's heroic efforts bear down upon them: walls of photocopying ten feet high; piles of paper stacks; thousands of flyers.

Yvette's smile widens.

Bananas

Is he still on earth? Maybe he should check the papers. Maybe he's no longer there. Maybe he's on mafia world.

While in his morning meeting with The Boss, he eats his banana and thinks about mafia world:

It isn't just his ex-friends and new associates. Last night he opened his door to two youths demanding goods under threat of vengeance. Gangster activity from the under-twelves. Extortion he calls it. 'Trick or treat,' they'd said.

Completely unprepared for Halloween, he'd complied with their request as is customary at this time of year, providing them with the most appropriate food he had – two ripe bananas, two of his best. They appeared quite happy with his gift even though their outward appearance didn't show it: slumped-shouldered they took off along the hallway, munching as they went, the potassium providing them a healthy alternative to chocolate.

After their departure, there had been two incidents. First, about an hour later, an egg had flown through his half open window and landed, unbroken, on the seat next to him in his lounge: a new event happening in his life which at the time had provided a welcome distraction from staring at green fabric. A minute later, a second egg, on a slightly higher trajectory, looped over his head and plopped down into his goldfish bowl (again unbroken). It was an enjoyable spectacle to watch from the comfort of his own living room, an interesting event happening to witness, he'd thought, until two more eggs simultaneously hit the closed portion of his window, splattering yellow yolk across his window pane.

At the window, though, anger had faded, turned to admiration. A very good throw, he had thought: to hit a window on the third floor required both accuracy and strength. It must have been the bananas.

The rest of the evening he'd spent picking out eggshell from woodwork, polishing windows and wondering whether the boys, seeing the rather obvious benefits of bananas to their throwing ability, would consume more of them. Altogether he was rather pleased with himself, with both his increasingly tolerant nature and his service to the youth of society.

'Well, what do you think?' his boss says, breaking him from yet another zone-out. The Boss looks at Adam as if he expects some kind of reply.

What had he heard? Adam delves into his subconscious, two F**CKERS and a TW*T: a low swear count. Very low for a conversation of this duration: he looks at his banana – it's almost finished.

'Sounds interesting,' Adam says after an overly long pause.

'You think so?'

'Yes.'

'Well, f*ck me. I thought you liked to close those deals yourself. I thought you'd think me a liability.'

The man is a liability. Adam now thinks himself one too. He is supposed to be listening to people more. Ever since he read that self-help book on listening, he'd made a conscious effort to listen, and yet twice now he'd agreed to something he was oblivious to. What is it this time?

'What?'

'So I'll join you at two on Friday and we'll F*CK the

B*ST*RDS.'

F*CK, indeed. First he agreed without his knowledge to block-booking Screen Seven. Now he's agreed to his boss coming along to a fake meeting.

'Also, what's this about a *Columbo* tape?' The Boss asks. Adam leaves without reply.

Outside in the corridor, he looks on the brighter side: the best way to tackle the problem, Adam thinks, is to ignore it, for now. He'll just deal with it on Friday.

The office kitchen is a squalid little room: dirty, messy and smoke filled; passing it on the way back to his desk, he overhears a conversation … about the television programme *Columbo*.

Earlier, in the lift, he thought he'd heard a similar conversation and assumed it was his imagination.

After a heated discussion with the Cinema Owner, and a few hours spent coming up with plot lines for his fictional Columbo video, he canvasses with Yvette.

Adam does not mention his problem with his boss: that it is looking likely that he'll not be attending the screening of *Lawless Heart* because of a fake meeting he is going to have to set up.

They start canvassing a few doors on from where they left off last time – a few doors from the house of Mrs Hargreaves.

Yvette knocks on the door of number thirty. A woman opens the door and upon seeing them, slams it closed.

'No – sorry, we're not religious,' a voice booms from behind the door.

Adam and Yvette stand on the doorstep, deliberating. Adam suggests they should knock again; Yvette is adamant they'd be wasting their time. 'Even if there has been a mis-understanding, that woman won't want to come to the film, free coffee or not,' she says.

They're disturbed by the sound of a note being slapped onto the door window.

It reads:

No Jehovah's Witnesses

22

Pride and Prejudice

In the spot where he stands during his tree-watching activities, there is a bucket of soapy water waiting for him. Next to the bucket, Yvette smiles while holding a mop ready for dunking. It is a false smile, a smile that contains a sense of displeasure.

He backs out of the kitchen slowly, stepping backwards one foot at a time until he feels the safety of carpet. Why she detests his blackbird-watching hobby is a mystery. Adam wonders whether he'll ever be able to watch them again from the comfort of his own flat. Still, he remains hopeful: not long ago she'd taken objection to him watching the green fabric covering his own television set, yet now she seems pleased to sit watching it for hours at a time, even when he's not there.

He resists the temptation to look for his feathered friend, spending his time this evening, instead, watching television with Sockball. Tomorrow at least, if cornered in a lift and forced to talk television, he'll have something to talk about apart from his fictional *Columbo* video.

———

'See there, that's a Kapok,' Sockball says, nodding at the television.

'Is it?'

'Yes, it only grows in the Brazilian rainforest.'

Of course, Adam has no way of checking this statement independently, and Sockball does not produce his book of trees to prove his statement. But one of Sockball's biggest attributes is that he does not lie, so Adam takes his word on the matter.

The smell from Sockball's orange-snap potpourri to-night is particularly pungent. Enough to make Adam's mouth water. Given Yvette's fondness for biscuits, he makes a mental note to get some as a peace offering.

After the nature documentary finishes, Sockball switches off the television and gives Adam the smile of a man who wants his guest to vacate his flat. Adam, who is more used to giving such a look than receiving it, is about to make his excuses and leave when they are disturbed by a knock at the door.

Adam watches as Sockball opens the door and greets his guest.

'Come on in,' Sockball says, 'I have been waiting.'

After the visitor enters, the door is left open briefly – a period of time long enough for an unwanted guest to leave – but Adam, intrigued by the tone of warmth and friend-ship in Sockball's voice, remains seated. Apart from himself and Yvette, what kind of friends does Sockball have, he wonders?

The visitor, a man large in girth and small in height, squelches up beside Adam on the sofa while Sockball flits to the kitchen to prepare customary welcome beverages. Adam feels a draughty, uncomfortable silence while their host is out of the room; the visitor and he sit far too close together, without talking to each other.

On arrival the refreshments produce within Adam the strongest pang of outrage he has had for some time: the tea is in a pot, the cups are good quality china, and the refreshments are accompanied by an almost full packet of biscuits.

Sockball proceeds to offer this new friend an orange snap!

They are offered to Adam too. He declines them out of principal: if such a biscuit is not offered to him in normal circumstances, he will not take one in these circumstances; he is not a biscuit monkey! He watches nonchalantly as the packet is placed on the table midway between himself and Sockball.

A minute passes before Adam caves in and starts helping himself.

'How is the rubber business these days?' Sockball inquires of his friend.

'Very good,' says the friend.

'And the textile business? How is the textile business these days?'

'Also very good. Very buoyant.'

'Good,' says Sockball. 'Good.'

The biscuits have a funny taste; Adam wonders if they have passed their sell-by. He eats a few more. Alarmed by the rapid decline in biscuit numbers, Sockball picks up the packet from the table and offers his friend another. The friend declines and the biscuits are put back in their original position.

Adam inspects them – the biscuits – and decides they would be better presented in a tin. Either they have passed their sell-by date, or they have been stored incorrectly – he examines the box: it's damp. Either way, this fails to explain why Sockball, his neighbour and friend, has failed to offer Adam an orange snap on any of his previous visits!

THUD.

'You see the problem?' says Sockball.

His friend shakes his head. 'You never were a good thrower, were you,' he says, then chuckles and looks at Adam. 'Umm,' he says, creasing his forehead.

'Never were a good thrower, were you,' his friend says again, before, more wildly and quite possibly on purpose, nodding at Adam.

As far as Adam can see, the socks had hit the point on the wall Sockball had been aiming at.

Adam had a desire to protect Sockball's reputation when it was attacked by Karen his almost-lover, and yet Sockball appears to see no value in defending himself. Sockball appears not to care about the slur on his undoubted throwing ability, and asks: 'Have you brought the prototype?'

The friend pulls a pair of socks from his briefcase and passes them to Sockball, who puts them straight on his now bare feet.

Sockball jumps up and down, then stops, then walks in a straight line towards the wall, pauses, and returns, bouncing as he walks. Standing back on his original mark, Sockball pulls the socks off and rolls them into a ball.

From a distance of five metres the ball of socks appears to Adam to be somewhat larger than normal: more circular, more spongy.

The socks are thrown ...

THUDD.

... bounce off the wall, the floor, and rebound back into his hands.

Quite …
THUDD.
… a remarkable …
THUDD.
… achieve– …
THUDD.
… ment.
THUDD.
Though …
THUDD.
… Annoy …
THUD.

'STOP!' Lunging off the sofa, Adam plucks the ball of socks from mid-air and lands flat-faced on the carpet. He suffers a minor carpet burn to his forehead and middle finger strain to his left hand. Much later, he'll blame this incident – the blow to the head – as a reason for his indecisive behaviour when ordering a pizza topping.

Sockball steps forward, unaware of injuries suffered, picks up the ball of socks and lobs it back to his friend, whom he now calls Michael, and tells him the socks aren't for him.

'They don't quite make the right noise. I'll stick to my plain socks,' he says.

An hour after the friend leaves, Adam tells Sockball that despite the insult from his friend, he believes Sockball is a good thrower.

'Yes, I know,' Sockball replies.

'Do not be concerned about the slight to your character,' says Adam, finding it hard to believe anybody could survive such harsh criticism.

'I'm not,' Sockball says. 'What do I care? What he thinks

is his business, not mine.'

Adam is perplexed: clearly Sockball and his friend were on good terms when they parted company; they got on well despite the insult. Sockball does not appear to be aggrieved in the slightest by his friend's attempts at ridiculing his sock-throwing ability.

The visitor this evening reminded Adam of his ex-friends, with their little undermining nuisances that individually had little effect but ended up pecking you into death; but Sockball remains unaffected by his friend's negativity.

'I have my beliefs about people and the things they do, but I do not comment upon them,' Sockball says a few minutes later, while watching another nature-cookery programme. Intermittently throughout the show, Sockball adds to his comments, muttering things like, *He'll let people be people, and let him be himself.*'

Adam remembers Sockball's tolerance of him being Alastair Sim. Tolerance isn't quite right: Sockball doesn't see anything to tolerate. Could it be that Adam himself is not as tolerant as he could be? Could it be that though his ex-friends are difficult, the answer to their flaws is toleration rather than abandonment? The thought makes Adam feel uneasy. Perhaps he has it wrong; *is* there anything to tolerate, for example? Could Sockball really be that unaffected by other people's actions? How exactly does Sockball feel about his Alastair Sim?

'What do you think of my Alastair Sim?' Adam asks.

'You are a lunatic,' says Sockball. 'Dressing up, walking around as ... Who did you say you were?'

'Alastair Sim.'

'As Alastair Sim—' (shrugs) '—A lunatic.'

Sockball switches off the television set, pulls a dictionary from his bookshelf, thumbs through half a dozen pages, and coughs.

'Lunatic: Person who is insane or very foolish or reckless.'

Adam must concede that walking around as Alastair Sim may come across to some as being *very foolish*.

'So we're both lunatics.'

'Me? No.' Sockball laughs. 'I'm normal.'

'Yes, in many ways, but playing Sockball isn't, is it?'

Sockball pulls off a sock.

'It's more common than you think.'

Adam attempts to hide his irritation.

'What is?'

'Sock-ball is … I'd say five percent of the population play it.'

Adam says nothing, hopes the conversation will move on.

'And it's a growing sport.'

But it does carry on.

'It's more of a winter sport. It's not so popular in the summer cos fewer people wear socks. Of course, people won't admit to it; it's got a bad reputation somehow. Same as tree-watching: it's just not trendy enough.'

23

High Noon

His third circuit takes him past the kitchen and tea-making facilities. He times his pit-stop: opening cupboard, retrieving mug, dropping teabag, adding boiling water (he'd switched the kettle on during his last circuit), retrieving garibaldi, and stop: ten seconds.

The pacing every morning puts him in a state of relaxation which lasts throughout the day. Some people start the day with yoga; he starts it pacing. The fact that he has to get out of bed an hour earlier to accommodate this experience does not make him a lunatic.

The course has evolved: it's longer, incorporates more obstacles, more muttering, more facial expressions and more props.

Through into the lounge, without stopping, and without looking down, he picks up a glass of water on his dining table.

Pace. Mutter. Sit. Eyebrows: 'Yes, inspector?'

There, what was so strange about that, he wonders? Definitely, he is not a lunatic.

Today, being Friday, he needs his pacing more than normal. This afternoon he and his compatriots will either save Screen Seven or have to deal with the reality of day trips to London.

Lunatic indeed – what man wouldn't pace under such conditions?

He leaves for work early, taking the direct route, a route which leaves him standing at the Silk Street traffic lights at five to nine. Deep in thought, he continues towards his office, thinking about his neighbour.

He was touched by Sockball: he really wasn't disturbed by that comment about his throwing abilities. Sockball didn't believe it to be a negative, or more precisely, didn't care whether it was a negative or not – he liked his friend in either case. And, yes, Sockball thinks Adam a lunatic, but not in a judgemental way, not in a negative fashion – plumped with bile or revulsion or blame. What have you got, what are you left with if you can't see the negative in a person: a good Frankenstein?

Has he discovered a Zen Master living along his corridor? Or is there something about throwing socks at a wall that gives you wisdom?

At work he shuts himself in a vacant office and starts to remove items of clothing.

THUD.

His socks miss the wall clock by inches, landing on a small cabinet, knocking assorted stationery to the floor.

THUD.

He has missed his Frankenstein friend: the one that's made only of the positive bits of his ex-friends' personalities.

THUD.

Even though Yvette's letter was a forgery, designed by his friends to ruin his love life, it did make a number of very important points: some of the negatives they attributed to him were true; like him being overly suspicious; like him zoning out and not listening; like him not knowing what colour is fashionable this summer.

Character flaws should carry a time limit; yes, he was like that in the past: suspicious, jealous, a bad listener.

THUD.

He may have been too hard on his ex-friends. Their misdemeanours too should have an expiry date.

THUD.

He wants to be a strong person all the time. A man that says he doesn't play games and means it. A man who'll take no nonsense from anybody; who'll stand up and be honest with his friends, his boss, his work colleagues. He wants to be more like his new friends: he wants more of Yvette's honesty and Sockball's open-mindedness. He'd like to be able to forgive negative attributes, like Sockball does. Would Sockball lie about a *Columbo* video? Would Sockball hide the fact that he spends the evenings watching green fabric and being Alastair Sim? Would Yvette? Would the heartthrob film star Clive Owen?

And he is that person, he can be that person part time: he can keep it going with his love life, introduce it to his friends, but it's not there all the time. He likes the man who was honest to his friends and the one who said he doesn't play games to Yvette, but is disappointed with the one who plays them with his boss and with his work colleagues.

Clive Owen, in those films, he is who he is, he just happens to be trendy while he's doing it. He doesn't hide who he is. Neither does Sockball. Nor his blackbird friend. And neither does Yvette. This just will not do.

At high noon, after taking several more requests for the *Columbo* Video, Adam walks calmly into the main office. Standing in the middle of the room, he pulls a chair from beneath a desk and surveys the office: it's busy – most people are there, including the boss.

Adam uses the chair to step onto the desk. This quickly gains the attention of his audience and makes him the focus of the room.

He takes a breath. Pauses. And takes another breath.

He's starting to think this isn't a good idea, this speech he's about to give, that it may be more appropriate to sing, some Elvis maybe? Or to dance, or to just get down off the desk and say nothing, walk away. He's wondering this when he becomes aware that he's already started to talk:

'As you are all aware. I told some of you recently that I had in my possession a *Columbo* video, and, I know it's going to be painful, for all of us, but … um, it doesn't exist.'

Silence.

He continues: 'No, um, what I need to say. What I mean to say is, that, I'm sure you can buy *Columbo* on video—' a collective sigh '—they exist out there, there are plenty of them. But I don't possess a copy. I just made it up.' He's quite good at public speaking normally, he just has to get to the point, say little, and leave them wanting more:

'Any questions?'

This time, though, giving this talk, he needs to make sure he gets the point across. The last time he'd made a speech – in the pub, saying goodbye to his friends – he thought he had made his point when quite clearly he had not: his communication wasn't clear enough.

'I'm sorry; I told somebody I had a *Columbo* video and I

don't. There is no video.'

More silence.

'I'm afraid I don't watch television much – the occasional wildlife cookery programme with my friend, Sockball, and that's it.'

Adam looks around the room, expecting distress but seeing indifference, as if they've not quite understood. Or don't care.

Aware that shock can have a delayed reaction that leads to anger and violence, he heads back to his office in search of his shoes and socks.

The wall clock reads one o'clock – one hour to the screening. There's still time for some last-minute photocopying. He ventures back into the main office.

'That was very brave of you,' The Boss says, cornering him in the corridor. 'Very gutsy.' His hands, clasped around Adam's shoulders now, squeeze ever so slightly as he grits his teeth. 'Well done.'

'You ready for our big meeting? – three o'clock – the big negotiation!' The Boss continues.

'Not going,' Adam replies with calm abandon. 'Going to the cinema instead.'

'But we've run out of parts,' The Boss says, confused. 'What is this, some big negotiation strategy – run away, make the f*ckers sweat, yeah?'

'No, I haven't been negotiating. I was going to place an order on Monday, normally. Like a normal person.'

'What?'

'I booked every ticket in the cinema. If I get enough people to go I make my money back and save the screening programme.'

'Wha …? You booked the cinema? Wha …? How much

you pay for the tickets?'

'Tickets? For the screening? Two grand.'

'But ... that sounds like a lot!' The look on The Boss's face is one of disappointment. Adam suspects it's directed not at him so much as at his negotiation skills. And he agrees with his boss: it is not a good deal. But it is important, to him, to keep his life going, to keep the bits of life he likes intact, so he is going anyway.

'I get it – you invited the suppliers yeah? Like corporate hospitality, and you don't want me to go. I won't F*UCK it up. I can help close deals, you know that right?'

So this is what happens when you tell the truth, Adam thinks: you're not believed. If he pushed it. If he lied, he could put the two grand costs on expenses, but he isn't going to play games. Adam explains this – that he is telling the truth – makes his excuses, leaves his befuddled boss, and makes his way to the photocopier to pick up his final flyers, relieved the fallout hadn't been worse.

At the photocopier, an engineer fixing a broken machine nearby corners him in a conversation. 'Why don't you like TV. What's your problem?' he asks.

Adam looks at his shoes and employs a variety of other tactics to show that he's not interested in engaging in this kind of conversation, but the man does not take his hints.

'You don't watch TV?'

'No. Not much.'

'On the other hand, you like the cinema!'

Adam's high-noon speech was supposed to clarify things, make life easier, but not playing games seems to have hurt this man's feelings. The man, who seems to be taking it as a personal insult, puts down his spanner and stands up.

'Is it possible to talk about something else?' Adam says.

'Sure. First, tell me what you've got against television.'

The big man – disgruntled, uneasy – stands looking directly at Adam: no longer selecting tools from his box, not fixing the other photocopier; he leans on Adam's machine, making it impossible for him to retrieve his flyers.

Adam tells the man that television for him does not provide the same stimulus as film. Plots unravel too fast, emotional angles are cramped, and he hates, really hates, having to wait for the next episode of anything: it's inferior in the things that matter despite the advantage that he can be sure he's watching it on his own. He says he likes watching films on television but doesn't subscribe to pay-TV, so except for the odd black and white film, it's rare for him to find something he hasn't already seen at the cinema or would like to see. And when there is something on – a good film, or a sitcom – there's the problem with the addiction. It's difficult to turn the thing off once it's on and he ends up watching reams and reams of drivel. Television drains his energy, film lifts it. He doesn't know why. It just does. Films on TV have been re-scaled; it's a different environment. They are two separate things.

'What. About. Football?'

'What about it?'

'I suppose I could watch it at somebody else's house,' the engineer says. 'Or in a pub. I just wanted to know how you did it, that's all. I've never met anybody who gave up television before. Thanks.'

The engineer grasps Adam's hand, and shakes it.

'Oh,' says Adam. 'Well … good. Oh, and my name's Adam.' A common opening line.

'Yes, I know, and I am Todd.'

Lawless Heart

Adam arrives early and helps the staff clean the screening room. The normal cinema snacks litter the floor: popcorn, pick and mix, coffee cups full of gooey chocolate crunch, which he has to scrape from a seat.

Afterwards, he lays, very carefully, a reserved sign upon each of the front row of seats, sits and waits.

It's not until ten minutes later – as the cinema starts to fill – that Adam feels angry: a couple spill some cola on the floor – a spot he'd cleaned moments previously. Walking towards them, intent on telling them to clean it up, he is distracted by the snacks: people walking in laden with snacks – he'd expected some snacks of course, he's a realist but there should be a limit. A snack limit. Next time there'll be a bouncer on the door, frisking on entry, taking confectionery in breach of the rules. He is about to query the entrants when the adverts start, and he quickly returns to his seat.

During the third advert, he notes that the lights are still on. What was he thinking, asking them to do away with the dimmer switch, a feature which has given endless enjoyment in the past? The Cinema Owner has found a way to adjust the lighting despite telling him it was impossible. Uneasy with the change, he feels a pang. He'll reinstate the dimmer next time.

He'd felt the pang earlier, witnessing changes to the coffee machine in the foyer: all the labels now read 'coffee'. Getting what he wanted was starting to disappoint. He had no idea charm and irritation were so closely connected.

The lights turn off in one hit.

A woman drops her popcorn. She vents her anger with the most inappropriate language for his cinema, though he's sure his boss would approve.

From behind him he hears The Boss laugh – at the poor woman's misfortune rather than her use of language. Adam was aware of the man following him to the cinema and thought he had lost him en route – an exercise which he now realises was pointless: there is only one cinema in this town; The Boss had obviously known where he was going.

'No. No. No,' Adam says, to nobody in particular.

The Boss picks up the reserved sign from the seat next to him and sits down.

'Where are they?' he says, presumably referring to the non-existent suppliers.

Adam points safely into the dark behind him. He doesn't want the fallout from his lying and skiving to happen during the film; much better, he thinks, if realisation dawns for his boss after the screening. Adam has, after all, been honest. He had told the truth already: if for some reason The Boss thinks he is lying – that actually he hasn't been skiving and has been in constant negotiation with the suppliers the whole time, and that this trip to the cinema is going to clinch the deal – then what is he supposed to do? He doesn't mind losing his job over the matter, but he won't cause a ruckus during the screening. He'll deal with the consequences afterwards.

As the film is beginning, during the opening credits, a spotlight is switched on.

A circle of light appears at the right-hand edge of screen and moves to the centre, highlighting Mr Geoff Porter. 'Quiet please; the film is about to begin,' he says, and then takes a bow. It's an introduction which had not been discussed beforehand, and that alarms Adam for a moment – until the opening credits finish.

Adam is not used to watching this type of film with so many others, apart, that is, from on his London excursions a few years ago. And it makes him feel uneasy. First, even though he sits at the front, he cannot pretend to be on his own: there is too much laughter. Worse than that, the laughter isn't in unison. It's as if each person in the screening room finds something individually hilarious – a private joke which only they can understand, which, to them, is the funniest thing they've ever heard but which skips Adam and the rest of the audience completely. Individually the audience laughs too loudly: it's just bad manners. He'd witnessed this phenomenon before, at an independent Soho Cinema, and thought it to be a London thing.

He notices how individual laughter is: he hears a laugh from his boss, from the Cat Man, from random audience members. He spends half the film waiting to hear Yvette giggle from the back of the cinema, but he hears nothing. It occurs to him that he has never heard her laugh in the cinema, that she's always quiet in Screen Seven.

When something genuinely funny happens Adam finds himself laughing on his own.

Long before the end credits it strikes Adam that this is the end of The Screen Savers, now the crusade has finished. There'll be no need to associate with the group any more. Finally he'll have the space in his life to concentrate on his big life plan.

The sadness he feels startles him. He'll miss them, his new friends. In a way he misses his old friends too, even though he sees them occasionally, when he's been abducted.

After the film, Adam scans the packed foyer. The group and most of the customers have stayed: Yvette mingles with the customers, passing round a tray of snacks; Mr Geoff Porter is courting the attention of a group of women in the corner of the room, talking politics and appearing somehow more interesting than normal; The Boss is talking with the Cat Man in confectionery. Occasionally he shoots Adam a worried glance or a wild-eyed excited smile while sticking up his big thumb.

Many of the people on their list had turned up: strangers he'd met at the door while supporting Yvette's act, and many, many, more youngster types whom he presumes are students enticed by the Cat Man and Mr Geoff Porter through their canvassing efforts.

In front of Adam an argument brews in the foyer – a couple standing nearby squabble over which was the best film, *Lawless Heart* or *Spiderman*.

'I said I liked *Spiderman*, OK? I said I preferred it to *Lawless Heart*. I DIDN'T SAY *LAWLESS HEART* WAS A PIECE OF CRAP, DID I?' the man shouts.

'I thought *Lawless Heart* was better,' the woman says.

'I know you thought it was better. All I'm saying is that I think *Spiderman* is a better film, that's all.'

'Yeah, but you dismissed me. I said I liked *Lawless Heart* and you said …'

It's something his relationship with Yvette doesn't have – conflict. He's even beginning to like the bottom slapping.

'So, what did you think was the best film? *Spiderman* or *Lawless Heart*?' Adam asks Yvette, who's now by his side, her snack-tray empty.

'I liked them both.'

'Me too.'

'I preferred *Lawless Heart* though.'

'Yes. Me too.'

Their conversation, Adam notes, has been much shorter than the other couple's. It'll save some space in his life, he thinks – not arguing will give him more time to do other things.

'Not bad, me old son,' says The Boss. 'Worth every penny.' He chuckles and sips coffee. 'Tell you what though, c**ts make up for it on the coffees, don't they. You know how much this cost me – have a guess.'

Adam doesn't say anything. The coffees are very cheap here.

'Seventy pence,' Yvette guesses correctly.

'Tell you what. I might come again. Why not. Bring my own flask next time.' Then, putting his hands on Adam's shoulders again, he says, 'Oh, err, and … don't get mad like usual – I didn't think you'd mind, but—' he tries to hold back a smile – 'I've just closed the deal.'

The Boss pauses for a moment, waiting for the obligatory congratulations, then continues when they are not forthcoming: 'Bit funny of the fella to bring his cat to a business meeting though, ain't it – the c*nt. I know you'd done all the prep, but I just wanted to have a go – and he said he'd give us a thirty percent discount.'

Maybe this is what happens when you stop lying: somebody else lies for you – the Cat Man in Adam's case. Now he will be indebted to both the fellow and his cat for pretending to be his suppliers. Of course the Cat Man's efforts rely on Adam brokering the same deal with the actual suppliers on Monday, but a thirty percent discount should be achievable, even at such short notice.

For now, Adam knows the programme at Screen Seven is saved. His crusade is over. There are enough people here for the Cinema Owner to keep the programme going.

Yvette, reading his mind, asks him what they do now.

Adam's response is immediate – he asks her out, to see a film at the three thirty on Thursday; but Yvette says she doesn't do dates.

'I don't do dates,' she says.

And Adam decides that there are some games worth playing.

24

Epiphany II

Six hours ago he had woken with an epiphany: a sudden realisation that he liked his friends; liked them enough, that is, to see them occasionally – a few times a year, say, with strict ground rules. Later on this morning – the epiphany bolstered with tea and coffee and messages of goodwill left on yellow post-it notes by Yvette – he'd thought 'like' too weak a word and upgraded it to a mixture of love and wanting-to-see-more-of. A rescaled epiphany, which applied, too, to ex-friends, work colleagues, and others he had difficulty in labelling.

There were reasons for it, this epiphany. Many. And that was six hours ago. Hours of working on his life – writing lists mainly – has led to one obvious course of action, and today he is going to take it … probably.

Pacing the flat as Alastair Sim he thinks about canapés; obviously they should have a biscuit base: savoury biscuits with a variety of toppings. Some of his ex-friends, he noted at the wedding abduction, have developed allergies to wheat (except when used in the brewing process), and thus an alternative is needed. A lucky dip cappuccino is a good idea, made by Yvette, and he could hold the whole event in the patisserie.

So this is what it's like to organise a party, he thinks, glowing with ... well, with pride.

There is much to do. First he calls into work and takes off an Epiphany Day – the last he is allowed this year – then he paces the flat as Alastair Sim.

Epiphanies are quite an occurrence these days, an epidemic if you will, and to accommodate the strain his company has granted their staff two epiphany-days a year to deal with the issue. He has a kind and sympathetic boss you may think, but understand this: THE NUMBER OF PAID SICK-DAYS HAS BEEN REDUCED BY A SIMILAR FIGURE.

In a break from pacing, he lies on his bed and adds to his list of guests to invite. Once his list is complete, he fills in party invites, puts the invitations into manila envelopes and lays them on top of his bed.

As is often the case after a rush of blood to the head, a cooling down period is required, an opportunity to pull out at the last moment if he decides he is doing something stupid. For this reason, he does not affix stamps but instead paces as himself around the kitchen, deliberating.

Have there been any changes to his lifestyle recently that would account for such a change in his thinking? Are there any other subconscious motives for inviting them over? Has there been a drastic change to his diet?

He looks at the ingredients listed on a tin of corned beef: beef, sugar, salt, sodium nitrate – nothing that would account for a mood-altering hormonal imbalance, even in the quantities that Adam now consumes it in (a mixture of tinned beef and crispbread now accounts for forty percent of his diet).

Have his recent dealings with The Screen Savers confused his thinking? Are there any other causal factors, and if so are they permanent? Or temporary; it's hardly wise to invite your ex-friends back into a new life only to find there is no room for them.

A lot more thought is required. He spends the rest of the afternoon pacing.

He's on his eighty-fourth lap when there's a knock at the door. He opens it instinctively, mid-stride, as he passes.

They push him back along the landing; a scuffle that finishes in the bedroom, where he ends up on his back, on his bed, tied up and gagged.

It's Steven's turn to pace now: up and down at the end of his bed. Steven looks mad this time, like a character from one of those films he likes, only more realistic.

'Now, we're only going to kidnap you if you stop with the Jehovah's Witness thing. Or at least you stop preaching it and trying to convert our families,' he says, flicking through the clothes in Adam's wardrobe. 'And if you let me have this.' He pulls out a light turquoise scarf.

Steven turns to Jay. 'Is this turquoise?'

Jay nods.

'OK,' Steven says. 'Stop the preaching. And give me this.'

Adam, still unable to talk due to being gagged, had been thinking about his ex-friends before they'd barged through the door, tied him up, thrown him on the bed and started to steal his clothing. He'd been thinking how interesting they had become, about their positive sides. A day out with them was not like it used to be, it's not your bog standard normal day out; it's become engaging, different, exciting, there is adrenaline involved. They had changed from aggressive lager-heads to pretend violent criminals in a few months.

Realising Adam is not replying for a reason, Steven ungags him.

'Thank you,' Adam says.

Karen is with the group this time. He notices her standing quietly in the corner, keeping quiet, distancing herself from the rough stuff.

'Hi, Karen.'

She smiles back at him – her mouth-hole cut in the balaclava is too large. It shows off her deep purple lipstick and reveals her unmistakable smile. It's a sultry look he would find appealing if not for a huge character deficit, and for Yvette.

'You play dirty. So do we,' says Steven, tightening his bindings.

'Me play dirty? You sent Karen to spy on me, sleep with me.'

Jay glances nervously over at Karen, who shakes her head a little too firmly.

Jay leaves the bedroom. Karen follows.

Adam and the remaining mafia ex-friends listen in as a few seconds later banging noises emanate from his kitchen – the sound of doors being slammed: his doors!

The noise level rises: a garbled mix of voices and clanging ring in from the kitchen. Listening more intently, Adam hears a new sound, of plates breaking, or is it, not … his mirrors!

'This must stop,' he says. Bristling with rage, he fights to free himself from his bindings. Quickly he runs out of energy and slumps back on the bed. He and the rest of the mafia clan return their focus to the sounds of battle raging along the corridor.

Adam's had hardly any contact with them for two weeks (since Karen's attempts at seduction), and since he discarded their lists he has been thinking only about their positive points.

Now, though, listening to the argument in his kitchen, he starts to recollect their bad ones.

Lying next to him on the bed is the pile of manila envelopes, the most prominent addressed to Steven, the man who is standing in front of him, at the foot of his bed, listening to the kitchen commotion.

Cautiously, so as not to arouse suspicion, Adam rolls slowly onto the envelope. Bound at the feet, arms strapped to his side, hands against his thighs, he rolls slowly onto his side, his front, his other side, his front again: A 360-degree rollover that he makes as quietly as possible and which, on completion, hides the letters from view.

In the two weeks since last contact with his ex-friends, his dislikes and irritations have left him; only a few hours ago he'd tried to remember their negative traits and could only come up with a few minor points. This morning, his ex-friends all of a sudden had become more positive.

It's good to have friends who understand your bad points, isn't it, he thinks. That letter they sent him pretending to be Yvette showed him how much they really knew about him.

He rolls back off the envelopes.

Steven's still at the door, listening to the commotion in the hallway. Some of the dialogue is audible – 'You were supposed to spy on him, NOT SLEEP WITH HIM,' Jay's voice booms through the wall.

Adam rolls back onto the envelopes.

Is it so bad to think you're in the mafia? Sockball can

put up with the negative in a disparaging-comment-making friend. Maybe Adam too can develop such a quality. Also, if Sockball can accept his Alastair Sim, couldn't he accept Steven's Al Pacino?

Without glancing towards Steven, he rolls off the envelopes.

The argument outside subsides; Steven opens the door a smidge to assess the aftermath.

Adam is still rolling off of and onto the letters.

With the passage of time, one so easily forgets a person's bad points. He does anyway. Character flaws, for him, are easy to spot and easy to forget. This is why he'd routinely need to look at those lists. And now that they're on the top of the rubbish tip with all his other possessions, he needs something else. He needs to see them every once in a while to remind himself that he doesn't want to see them. He rolls off the letters.

The abductors, standing at the bottom of the bed, are watching him. Jay and Karen are there too, holding hands now, also watching.

The seesawing action of rolling backwards and forwards has dispersed the invitations: some of them have attached themselves by static to his chest, the rest are randomly scattered about the bed and floor.

'We really mean it this time,' Steven says, pulling Adam out of his daydream. 'This is your last chance: stop preaching religion, give me this scarf, come and have a beer, and get a tattoo. Look.' He shows Adam his arm – the tattoo on it reads *'No Surrender'*.

'I don't drink alcohol.'

'What? Is this part of that Jehovah's Witness shite?'

He can't go back. His life had changed since he had split from the group. It may seem less interesting from the outside, less boozy, less partying, less socialising, more alone time pacing the flat being Alastair Sim, but he likes it. He prefers his life now, even without the excitement of being occasionally kidnapped and forced to drink pints of Guinness literally at knife-point. He suspects he isn't strong enough to be himself while being with them. There is too much history.

'Yes, that's right. I am a Jehovah's Witness. That's why I don't drink.'

'Is that why you hate me – because I'm gay?'

'I don't hate you and I don't care that you're gay,' he says, then remembers that Jehovah's Witnesses are anti-homosexual. He's not sure if they're teetotal.

The other men and Karen – none of whom are now wearing their balaclavas – have a delayed, silent reaction to Steven's news. Adam notes this, surprised the group hadn't known about Steven's sexuality. He feels like walking over and giving Steven a hug. His ex-friends hadn't had any real problems over the last six months, no real revelations to bring them together.

'Nobody cares about that any more. We never did.' He uses *we* in the context of the group of old friends in the room, even though the others hadn't been aware of it. There's much nodding and grunting in support for what's being said.

'No. But my mother does.'

Steven's mother, a Mrs Hargreaves, had known of her son's homosexuality for a long time. Adam knew this for a fact: he remembers visiting them one summer, being there for support when Steven had told her the news.

'Ever since she's become a Jehovah's Witness. Ever since you went round with your leaflets. Preaching. Converting. And … Why did you do that?'

'Leaflets? We didn't take anything. If she's converted, it's not our fault.'

He still wants to get up and give Steven a hug. He would too, if he could move his arms or legs. He wants to be there even for his ex-friends when times are hard. He'd planned a complete exile for a year or so, until he felt good within his new life, and then he'd wanted to be there – only for the real critical moments in life, those transcending birthdays, marriages and Christmas – and treat past friends like Steven as if they were loved, distant relatives he never sees.

He is not tempted to give up his new life, not tempted to say, 'Let's forget about it and all go to the pub and get pissed like we used to years ago', and go to their birthdays and garden parties.

'We were just canvassing to save the cinema's scr—'

'For us abducting you a couple of times, you turned our families into Jehovah's Witnesses?' Steven interrupts, pulling out a large sharp knife.

'Leave him alone,' Jay barks.

Jay makes a movement towards Steven, but doesn't stop him.

'You can fuck off then!' Steven shouts.

He cuts the ropes binding Adam.

The ex-friends leave.

Later, he wonders if it had all been another game, his last visit from the gang – an advanced game of emotional blackmail. He wonders if they might turn up again and continue playing.

But they never do.

25

Epilogue: Three Months Later

Three more months of the programme at Screen Seven and numbers decline; The Screen Savers disband; Adam and Yvette, disappointed at first, start screening old black and white films in the patisserie.

The Cat Man and Mr Geoff Porter, hooked on coffee, more aggressive in their plight, continue to strive for the resurrection of Screen Seven.

They form The New Screen Savers.

Epilogue II: Six Months Later,
A News Report

Two masked gunmen hijacked a West End cinema today taking a screening room hostage. Cinemagoers were forced, at gunpoint, to view a director's cut of *Buffalo '66*.

Despite their ordeal, many customers claim *Buffalo '66* was an OK film, much better than they'd expected. The pair, who call themselves The New Screen Savers, are still at large.

The cinema will be offering a full refund on production of ticket stubs and purchase of large popcorn.

Epilogue III: Nine Months Later

The New Screen Savers have been arrested and sentenced to six years' imprisonment. They are currently serving their sentences in a high-security prison, where they run the film society.

THE END

THE SCREEN SAVERS

BOOK EXTRAS

12A

BRYAN ROMAINE

**Did you like *The Screen Savers*?
Want to read more?**

Want to know how Sockball invented his
sock-throwing game?

Sign up to my newsletter at the link below and
receive a free ebook copy of
The Screen Savers Book Extras.

Book Extras include:
Deleted Passages
An update from Sockball
The story behind the book cover
And more

Sign up here:
www.bryanromaine.com/tss-extras

Signing up to the newsletter means you will find out
about giveaways, sneak peeks, geek-outs and will receive
updates on my projects along with other cool stuff.
I take your privacy seriously and you can unsubscribe at
any time.

About The Author

I have been writing for a number of years. I completed the first draft of this novel, *The Screen Savers*, in 2000. I had promising feedback but did not get published. I also widely submitted the project in 2012/13, again without success, and am thus grateful for the opportunity to self-publish through this internet thingy.

I also shoot short films and write feature-length screen-plays. My short films have appeared in a number of festivals and film competitions including the New York Friars Club Comedy Film Festival, which screened my comedy short film *Chess Clock Timer*. This film (which contains adult themes), along with some of my other short films and sketches, can be seen on my website—

www.bryanromaine.com

—and YouTube channel:

www.youtube.com/bryanromaine

Thank you for reading *The Screen Savers*.

Bryan Romaine

Links

To be kept up to date with new book, film, sketch and other projects please sign up to my newsletter. You will find out about giveaways, sneak peeks, geek-outs, updates and other cool stuff.
www.bryanromaine.com/newsletter

You can find out more information about
The Screen Savers here:
www.bryanromaine.com

For additional fun, for various benefits, and to make me look popular, follow me on my other social media sites too – including these ones:
www.facebook.com/BryanRomaineAuthor
www.twitter.com/bryanromaine
www.youtube.com/bryanromaine
www.instagram.com/bryanjromaine

Reviews

Getting a novel noticed is difficult for an indie author. Being reviewed helps enormously. If you liked *The Screen Savers*, it would be great to see your comments on the website of the bookstore from which you purchased the novel. You can also find links to review/discuss/spread the word about this novel on my website.

Made in the USA
Middletown, DE
07 February 2019